Immortal Longings of Oz

Immortal Longings of Oz

Immortal Longings of Oz

By Paul Dana
Founded on and Continuing
The Famous Oz Stories
By L. Frank Baum
Royal Historian of Oz
Illustrated by Jaun Raza

THE ROYAL PUBLISHER OF OZ
New York

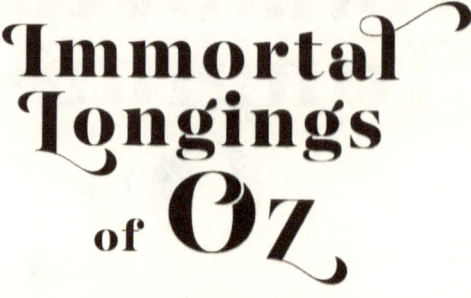

Immortal Longings of Oz

Being the Further Adventures of Ojo and Button-Bright,
and Their Dealings With the Rulers of Noland and Ev,
Where They Encounter Rebellion, Treachery,
and International Intrigue

R P O

The Royal Publisher of Oz

August 2019

The Royal Publisher of OZ

**For a timeline of the Oz series,
head over to The Royal Timeline of Oz
www.oztimeline.net**

Immortal Longings of Oz

10 9 8 7 6 5 4 3 2 1

ISBN: 978-1-7337151-5-7

The Royal Publisher of Oz
1085 Frances Dr., Valley Stream, NY 11580

Book design by Joe Bongiorno with Marcus D. Mébès
Printed by Lulu publishing: www.lulu.com

Printed in the United States of America
First edition: August 2019

This Book Belongs To:

_____

_____

_____

THE ROYAL TIMELINE OF OZ
WWW.OZTIMELINE.NET

LIST OF CHAPTERS

A LETTER FROM OJO THE LUCKY

Dear Readers,

This morning in the Emerald City, Trot asked me what it feels like to have magic powers. "You and Button-Bright used to be just like Shaggy and Betsy and the rest of us," she said. "And now, between the two of you, you have enough magic to do almost anything!"

Almost anything? Not by a long stretch! It's true that we've picked up certain kinds of magic that come in handy sometimes. Traveling is faster and easier with Button-Bright's Yookoohoo transformations, and my fairy magic has gotten us out of one or two tight spots. Still, as I told Trot, a boy's magical powers are only as good as his thinking powers—and our thinking powers haven't improved one bit. We actually get into more trouble now than we did before!

What happened in Ev is a great example. We thought we understood what was going on there, but it turned out we didn't, and that's when things really got mixed up. Apparently people have strong feelings about matters like immortality, Queen Lurline, and the Magic Eggs. Thank goodness we got help from folks who are a lot smarter than we are, such as King Bud and his sister Fluff, along with the royal family of Ev and a jarring friend who turned up right in the middle of everything. We learned a lot that we wish we'd known before we started.

We learned another thing, too. International diplomacy (whatever that is) may not be our strong suit.

Please enjoy the story! Everyone from the Emerald City sends their best!

Affectionately,

OJO

Ojo the Lucky

CHAPTER ONE

THE DUNGEONS OF EV

The spiral stairway to the old dungeons looked even grimmer than Princess Runa had imagined. Cold sweat beaded the stone walls and icy draughts found their way down Runa's collar. As the guards pushed her down, step by slippery step, the very air she breathed seemed to grow thicker and colder. She had never seen the place, but she and her sister had learned about it from their father, King Evardo.

"Ev never had a crueler king than your grandfather," Evardo had told his daughters many years ago, when they were still young girls.

That grandfather was the late King Evoldo of Ev, now openly referred to by everyone as Mad Evoldo. Runa and her sister had learned why. More than sixty years ago, Mad

Evoldo had burdened the whole Land of Ev with oppressive laws and ruinous taxes, as well as devising cruel punishments for those who spoke out against him. The poor Wheelers had suffered most of all. Mad Evoldo had enslaved as many Wheelers as he could, banished others from the city of Evna, and locked the best and brightest in dungeons.

Then he'd drowned himself in the sea. That should have been a matter for celebration, but unfortunately it had left the country with no one to govern it. Mad Evoldo had sold his whole family to the Nome King (in exchange for a long life, ironically), and his wife and ten children had been transformed into ornaments. It was only when the good people of Oz conquered the Nome King and disenchanted the royal family that a new king had come to the throne. This was Evardo, then only sixteen years old, yet determined to right his father's many wrongs. He had opened the dungeons and freed the suffering Wheelers. Then he had sealed the dungeons—forever, he had promised.

Now, more than a half century later, those same dungeons opened their doors for Evardo's beloved daughter Runa.

A vicious kick from behind sent Runa lurching against the curved wall. With her manacled hands she could do nothing to save herself, and she bumped and slid down five stone steps before she succeeded in getting her feet underneath her. The guards guffawed.

"Be glad you're not one of your Wheeler friends," one taunted. "You'd have rolled right down to the bottom. A little heap of broken bones, that's what you'd be."

"Now keep moving!" snarled the other. "You can rest when you get to your cell."

"My father will help me!" Runa retorted.

The guards only laughed at her. "King Evardo will never help anyone again," they said.

"He will! The Red Jinn will find a way to wake him."

"Hah! Your friend the Red Jinn hasn't woken him yet, I hear. And why's that? Either he doesn't want to or the spell's too tough for him. Your sister Eviret is Queen Regent now, and the dungeon is where she wants you. Here's your cell. Cozy, isn't it?"

The cell had clearly been intended for Wheelers. It contained neither seat nor bed, for the prisoner would have been expected to curl up like a dog. An ancient, filthy food tray sat on the bare floor like a dog's supper dish, a relic of bygone years when Wheelers had been treated like sub-human brutes.

Reforming this injustice had only been the beginning of King Evardo's great dream. He and his queen, the former Princess Fluff of Noland, had spent half a century reconciling the disparate peoples of Ev and inspiring humans and Wheelers to live together in peace and harmony. Today that dream lay in ashes. Out of nowhere an enchanted sleep had felled the hale old King. Power had passed into the hands of their elder daughter, now Queen Regent Eviret, who had made it her mission to roll back her father's reforms. Her stubborn younger sister, Princess Runa, had fought her every step of the way—but in vain.

Hard heels were heard outside Runa's cell. The guards fell silent and stepped aside.

"Oh, this *awful* place!" moaned Queen Regent Eviret as she tripped into view, holding her stylish gown above her ankles. At forty years old, she still dressed like a teenager on her way to her first ball. "You really should be ashamed of yourself, Runa, making me come down here when you *know* how easily I catch cold. You never think of *me*."

One of the guards took the hint and lent her a handkerchief. Eviret blew her nose into it, then returned it to the guard.

"And that's not the worst," she went on in her high, girlish voice. "You've been bad, Runa, very bad indeed. I wish I knew what you were *thinking* in that mean little head of yours. *What* would Father say?"

"Father would never have put me in here," said Runa.

"No, I don't suppose he would. Dear, sweet, silly old Father couldn't *bear* to punish anyone, could he? He didn't understand how *awful* people really are. And that's why things got *so* terribly out of hand. *No* one could have regretted it more than I when the enchanted sleep took him. But after all, he *was* seventy-six years old, wasn't he? He *needed* to retire."

"He did not need to retire!" Runa argued. "He was strong and fit and as sharp as ever."

Runa did not know that the people of Ev tended to live longer and stay fitter than folks do in the Outside World, but she did know that, on that final, fatal morning, King Evardo had looked and acted much as he had at age fifty. He had laughed and joked at breakfast, played a few rounds of badminton with Runa, then gone off with Queen Fluff to manage his kingdom. It had been a shock to everyone when he abruptly fell asleep and could not be wakened. It had also been a shock when the law of Ev placed Eviret squarely on the throne.

"Father wasn't as perfect as you think, Runa," Eviret said piously. "He and Mother made a lot of mistakes. Perhaps it's just as well that this *sad* affair has given me the opportunity to tidy up here in Ev." She gave her head a little shake, so that her golden hair tumbled becomingly about her shoulders.

"Stop preening," Runa said in disgust. "There's no one to notice."

The Queen Regent gave an extravagant sigh. "Typical little sister. *Such* a killjoy. When will you learn that there's more to life than your silly *causes*? But you never fooled me with your *do-gooding*, though you may have fooled Father. I had you brought here today because of certain *documents* that Uncle Evington found hidden in your room. Just imagine my *shock* when I read them. Runa, you *conspired* to steal Father away from me! You and Mother and Aunt Evanna *smuggled* him up north to the Red Castle. Do you deny it?"

"I don't," shrugged Runa. "Why should I? They're all beyond your reach now. The Red Jinn hasn't broken the spell yet, but at least he'll save Father from you."

"From *me?*" A tear trickled down Eviret's rouged cheek. "You make me sound like a *monster*. I would *never* hurt Father. I love him from the bottom of my *heart*! I only want to *protect* him."

"Yes—from anyone who might break the spell you put on him! That's why we had to get him out of here. We were the only ones who could."

This was true. Most of King Evardo's nine sisters and brothers had long since married and moved to other countries. The only ones left were Evington, who commanded the Palace Guard, and Evanna, who had headed Evardo's Council. Everyone said that Princess Runa took after her Aunt Evanna—loving, stubborn, and passionate in her pursuit of justice. Eviret, by contrast, took after Mad Evoldo, the grandfather she had never met.

During the first terrible months of the mysterious sleeping spell, when the eyes of the world had been upon her, Queen Regent Eviret had made a great show of trying to wake her enchanted father. She had summoned every quack doctor and soothsayer from miles around to conduct lengthy examinations and mumble useless charms. But would she summon the one real magician in Ev, as Fluff and Evanna had urged so strenuously? She would not, and no one doubted the reason. It was Eviret herself who, though unwilling to destroy her father outright, had first contrived to enchant him and then taken the throne in his stead.

And unconscious he had remained, month after month. He needed neither food nor water to sustain him in his magic sleep. His silvery hair and beard did not grow, his limbs seemed to retain their strength, and he breathed at a slow and steady rate. But nothing roused him. Nothing ever would, Fluff and Evanna had decided, unless they could take him to his good friend the Red Jinn. This the Queen Regent absolutely forbade.

So a desperate plan had been born. Its success had been far from assured, and if the conspirators had been discovered they would have gone to prison. Miraculously, however, it had all worked. Runa had managed to distract the guards in the dead of night. On the backs of two loyal Wheelers, Fluff and Evanna had spirited the sleeping King away through the darkened corridors to a hidden passage known only to the kings of Ev and their most trusted advisers. Under the very walls of the palace it led, and out to the city streets. There, by means of a wagon from the Royal Theater, loaded up as if for a tour of the provinces, the helpless King had been smuggled out of the city and north to the Red Castle.

Eviret had been furious. Unable to find the culprit, she had blamed everyone. Poor Runa had watched while the city of Evna became a fortress, guarded night and day by Uncle Evington's armed guard. She had watched while Evna's Wheelers were once more reduced to slavery. Yet for two years Runa herself had managed to escape detection. Until now.

18

"Who else helped you?" Eviret demanded. "That's what I want to know. You and Mother and Aunt Evanna can't have done it on your own."

"No one helped us," Runa insisted. "We did it all."

"Really? Well, perhaps you'll change your mind about that after a few days down here. But I *could* make a guess or two in the meantime. No doubt your Wheeler *friends* had a hand in the business. Or rather, a *wheel*!" A sudden braying laugh erupted from the Queen Regent's perfectly painted lips. "And now you're plotting to get the Wheelers out of Evna too! I will *not* have my Wheelers *smuggled* out from under my nose. Who will draw my *carriage* if they're allowed to escape? I *trusted* all of you once, out of the goodness of my *heart*, and look what happened! My father was *kidnapped* and bundled off to the Red Castle. *Everyone* knows the Red Jinn must have cast that sleeping spell on King Evardo!"

"You lie!" cried Runa heatedly. "It was you who cast that spell!"

More tears appeared in the Queen Regent's blue eyes. "You're all *against* me!" she wailed. "Even my own *sister*. Why do you *hate* me so? Yet in spite of *everything* I keep on trying. Goodness knows why. Certainly *I* get nothing out of it. This endless sacrifice is for *Ev*, all for *Ev*. But you don't understand, you and Mother and the rest. If I hadn't taken a hand in the matter, you would have raved on and on about *rights* and *compassion* till the Wheelers had murdered us all in our beds!"

19

She no longer seemed to be addressing Runa. Rather, it was with an unseen inner audience that she debated now.

"Wheelers! Those brutes, those savages who *stole* our family's chance at immortality. What was Queen Lurline *thinking* when she gave immortality to *them?* Who were they? *Nobody*, that's who. Less than nobody—a pack of rude, ungrateful, barbarous *servants*. While we, *we* were the royal family of Ev! The gift of immortality should have been *ours!*"

"That was more than two-hundred years ago," Runa pointed out for what felt like the two-hundredth time. "If Queen Lurline had given our family immortality, you and I wouldn't be talking about it right now. Our ancestors would still be ruling Ev, and we might never have been born at all."

A momentary spasm of confusion seemed to blur the Queen Regent's certainties. *"The gift of immortality should have been ours!"* she cried out again, as if repetition alone could silence every objection. "Grandfather understood. Evoldo the Mad, they call him now. But he's the only one who *did* something about it. He went to the Red *Jinn*, he went to Queen *Zixi*, he even went to *Mo*, where everyone is completely *insane*. He sent messages to Glinda of *Oz* and to that *idiotic* Queen Lurline! Not *one* of them would give him immortality. Are we no better than Mother's *peasants* in Noland? *That's* why Grandfather finally went to the Nome King. *That's* why he sold his wife and children. Blame *Lurline*, blame the Red *Jinn*, but *don't* blame poor Grandfather, who ended his tragic life in the *sea*."

"Not a moment too soon," muttered Runa.

"Oh, you just want to talk!" sniffed her exasperated sister. "I know what I know. Grandfather died in *misery*, but *I* won't. Somehow, some way, I *will* become immortal. And your misbegotten Wheeler *friends* will learn their place once and for all."

"Oh? And what happens when Father wakes up from his enchanted sleep?"

The Queen Regent stared at her sister, her mouth a perfect O of surprise.

"Why, then he'll be king again," she said at last, shrugging her shoulders. "But *that* hardly seems likely, does it? Poor Father has been asleep for three *years* now. Jinnicky hasn't been able to wake him. No, I fear King Evardo will never see the light of day again.

"And neither will *you*, Runa, so long as you persist in your *stubbornness*. But I think you're wiser than that. I think you'll tell me what I want to know. I'll find out what *all* of you are thinking and talking about behind my *back*—the mean, cruel things you say about *me!* I'll read your letters. My spies will overhear your conversations. You'll have no more secrets from me, no, not a single *thought!* And then your Wheeler friends will find out how much like Evoldo the Mad I really am."

"Someone's sitting in Grandma Natch's rocking chair," said Ojo. "And it isn't Grandma Natch!"

The two swallows—or rather, the two boys magically transformed into swallows—had just swooped down over the forest and into the clearing where Grandma Natch's house stood, but now they veered off in alarm and lit upon a tree branch with a good view.

Ojo and Button-Bright had spent the last couple days resting up here in the far northern reaches of Oz. They hadn't seen a soul other than local birds and squirrels, perhaps a raccoon or two, and of course Button-Bright's beloved Grandma Natch. They had prowled the purple depths of Gugu Forest, sometimes on two feet, sometimes on four; they had splashed through its streams and ponds, sometimes in their own boyish skins, sometimes in fish form. It had been a much-needed holiday for them.

Now they were expecting an important visit from two dear friends. In swallow form they'd been circling the skies all morning, keeping a sharp eye out for two familiar figures seated on a small, swift cloud—Onna Val's traveling cloud, as she called it.

The sky remained empty. Down below, however, a complete stranger sat hunched in Grandma Natch's rocking chair. Unheard of! She wore a red skirt and a red blouse, with a red shawl pulled tightly over her ancient shoulders. Beside her sat a small red suitcase and a red cane. Strands of white hair showed under her tall hat. On her lap perched a bowl of soup or stew, which she poked at suspiciously with a spoon. Of Grandma Natch there was no sign.

The strange old lady talked to herself in a peevish, piercing voice that carried right across the clearing. "I don't trust this magic soup," she fretted. "What if it burns my tongue? Why, it might make me scream out loud. And then if there are fierce animals nearby, they might hear me and come prowling out of the forest." She peered at the purple trees and pulled her red shawl even tighter around her shoulders. Her hands were gnarled and blotched. "And if the animals have big appetites," she went on, "they might devour me for lunch! I'm sure they will. That's what comes of eating magic soup."

This dreadful prospect galvanized her. She drew a deep breath, opened her mouth as wide as it would go, and shouted at the top of her lungs, "Young woman! Young woman, I know you're there! This soup is too hot! I want cold soup, do you hear me? Cold soup!"

She banged her spoon on the bowl. No one replied. No one came.

"Every wild animal in the forest must have heard that," observed Ojo.

"And they're probably running away as fast as they can," said Button-Bright. "Nobody, but nobody has ever sat in that chair except Grandma Natch."

Indeed they had not. For more than two-hundred years Button-Bright's grandmother, a Yookoohoo enchantress, had lived right here in the Gillikin Country of Oz. No one else stepped into this clearing without her say-so, and no one else had ever sat in the rocking chair that stood on her verandah. Until now.

"Look how old that lady is!" marveled Button-Bright. "She's much older than Grandma Natch. I didn't know anyone could be that old. How do you suppose she got here all the way from the Quadling Country?"

Both boys knew she must be a Quadling because she wore red clothes. Here in the wild northern country of the

Gillikins, purple prevailed both in nature and in fashion. Grandma Natch never wore anything else and Button-Bright had taken to doing the same. This ancient stranger stood out like a sore Quadling thumb.

"Cold soup!" she shouted, banging her spoon again.

"I suppose we'd better get to the bottom of this," Button-Bright said grimly.

He spread his wings, soared down to the ground, and transformed himself to his natural boyish shape. He also transformed his best friend Ojo, who had come with him. They would face this new danger, as they faced all dangers, together.

"Aha!" cried the old lady. "Finally you show up! It's about time. My soup is too hot and the young woman who made it has disappeared."

"What young woman?" asked Ojo.

"Purple dress. Gray hair. Calls herself Natch. She turned a stone into scalding hot soup and now she expects me to eat it. At my age! Come to think of it, she could turn *me* into soup. She could turn me into a stone, too. Or a stick! If she does that, I won't be able to talk anymore; and if I can't talk, how will you find out what I want done? I won't have it, I tell you! I won't, I won't, I won't!" With that she threw her bowl right across the clearing. After it came the spoon.

The two boys ducked. Hot soup spattered across the ground behind them. Had this ancient, indignant creature really called Grandma Natch a "young woman?"

Button-Bright decided he could at least solve the soup problem. Wrong! The first bowl he whipped up with his Yookoohoo magic was too cold for the old lady's taste and would, she said, turn her belly into an ice cube. The next was too salty and would give her indigestion. And so it went, until the bowl had been transformed thirteen times in rapid succession. At last she got a soup she could stomach, albeit grudgingly, and she began spooning it up. Button-Bright and Ojo watched with wide eyes. The absence of Grandma Natch filled them both with apprehension.

"You haven't asked my name," the old woman groused. "I'm Dame Zanket. That's one thing I haven't forgotten yet. But what will happen if I do forget it? Probably I'll totter out into the road and forget where I'm going. And then I'll fall into a ditch and break all my bones. And then I'll lie there forever, unable to move or speak, and no one will even care! And then—"

She seemed to have forgotten that she'd somehow made her way all the way across Oz, through goodness knows what perils, to the remotest and most unlikely corner of the Gillikin Country she could possibly have picked.

Ojo interrupted her catastrophic imaginings. "Where are you trying to go?"

"Why, here, you foolish boy!" Dame Zanket exclaimed. "This very spot!"

"But why?" asked Button-Bright.

CHAPTER TWO

"To see you! You're the Yookoohoo everyone's talking about, aren't you? Of course you are. And the other one is your magical friend. You're going to help me. You're going to find me a home in Ev. You're going to fix it up all nice and comfortable. And then you're going to take me there to live!"

So that was it. Button-Bright and Ojo exchanged knowing glances. Ever since they'd acquired their magical powers—the transforming power of a Yookoohoo, in Button-Bright's case, and in Ojo's the more mysterious and encompassing power of a Magic Egg—the two boys had become something of a travel agency. In the immortal Land of Oz most people could choose the age at which they wished to stop growing older, and they could remain that age for as long as they wished. But there were a few, victims of the fairy Lurline's capricious enchantment, who had no choice in the matter. So long as they remained in Oz they could not age a day, or even a minute. They could not escape from Oz either, for Oz was surrounded by a Deadly Desert that none could live to cross on foot. For those who liked the age at which they were trapped, this was all well and good. Others, however, had lived lives of great discomfort and inconvenience for over two-hundred years.

A handful of these unfortunates had recently persuaded Button-Bright and Ojo to transport them over the Deadly Desert and into the neighboring country of Ev, where they could escape the spell of immortality that held them in thrall. But finding homes for the emigrants was becoming more difficult. A good friend in Ev (herself the daughter of a woman from Oz) had been willing and happy to accommodate one small family and had even found neighbors willing to take more. That had exhausted all known options. Where to turn next?

The problem loomed large because two new "clients" had presented themselves. These were none other than Onna Val and Jandilay, the exact pair whose cloud-borne arrival was expected this very morning. Onna Val and Jandilay were beloved friends and fellow adventurers who had helped the boys through many difficult moments. Now that they wanted to grow up and live full mortal lives, Button-Bright and Ojo were determined to find them the best possible place in Ev. But where? And with whom?

Now here came Dame Zanket—yet another "client" for international relocation.

"Dame Zanket," said Ojo. "Why on earth do you want to start getting older again? You're already about as old as can be."

"I'm older than anyone you'll ever meet!" Dame Zanket boasted. This was untrue, but she did look it. "I've been old for more than two-hundred years! My joints creak, my toes cramp, and my back won't straighten up. I'm tired. I want out!"

"That doesn't make sense," said Ojo. "There's no disease in Oz. How can you be sick?"

"I didn't say I'm sick!" stormed Dame Zanket. "I said I'm old! Getting sick is what natural folks do in natural countries where everybody grows up and gets old and dies. Oz used to be a natural country back in the old days. And me, I was a sick old woman about to die. I had no quarrel with that. I was ready to go. And I would have gone, too—but that fairy Lurline had to cast her immortality spell on all of us. She didn't get *my* permission, I tell you that! Now I can't get sick and I can't die and I'm mad as a hammerhead!"

The boys had heard nothing like this before. They had no idea what to make of it.

Dame Zanket was opening her red suitcase. Out came an ancient, discolored, crackling bundle of paper. "I kept a diary!" she cried, waving the bundle triumphantly. "A diary of my final years. Or what should have been my final years. I brought it with me when I moved to Flutterbudget Center. Listen here." She squinted at the topmost sheet of paper and read aloud in tones of deathless drama, "*I start this diary because no one wants to hear about my maladies anymore. Who can I talk to? Why, the one party that can't walk away. That's you, dear Diary. Let's start with the heart trouble. That's enough to do me in right there—and I wish it would hurry up and do it. But what really keeps me up at night is the way my innards—*"

"All right, all right!" interrupted Ojo. "We believe you, Dame Zanket. You were sick. It was awful. But now you're well, aren't you? Oz magic keeps you that way."

"Be quiet, you! I haven't even gotten to the good part," Dame Zanket protested, thumbing through her bundle. "Here's the section where my lungs—"

"No, please!" Button-Bright implored. "Dame Zanket, if we take you to Ev, all this sickness you're talking about will come right back. You don't want that, do you?"

"That's exactly what I want!" screeched Dame Zanket. She seized her red cane in her fist and thumped it forcefully on the verandah floor. Her wizened face was pink with rage. "If I can't get sick, I can't die. And if I can't die, there's no way out. And if there's no way out, I'm stuck this way forever. It's intolerable, I tell you! I won't stand for it!"

"Now, you don't want to die," said Ojo. "Not really. No one does."

"I do too!" Dame Zanket yelled. "Oh, you young things don't understand! Your eyes work fine, you digest your food, you sleep all night and wake up ready for anything. What do you know about getting old? Nothing! And it's not my job to explain it to you. All I want is to go to Ev. Until you take me there I will not budge from this rocking chair!"

Not budge? Grandma Natch would have fits. And where *was* Grandma Natch? This was the question that worried Button-Bright most of all. "Well," he said doubtfully. "We plan to go to Ev in the next day or two. We have friends who want to move there. I suppose you could come with us."

"Do you have a place all ready for me?" Dame Zanket demanded.

"Not yet. But I'm sure we could find something—"

"NO! No, no, no, no, no!" The verandah shook with the thumping of the red cane. "Are you mad? Go all that way when I don't know what's waiting for me at the other end? Why, you'll have me sleeping up in a tree! Or down in a ditch! Or in some barn full of cows and goats! No, you go on ahead and get it all set up. *Then* I'll move—and not one minute sooner!"

The look in her eye brooked no argument. Button-Bright groaned.

"We have got to find Grandma Natch," he said fervently.

CHAPTER
THREE

ON THE WRONG SIDE
OF GRANDMA NATCH

The entrance to Grandma Natch's burrow, concealed under a clump of purple sage behind the house, had a quiet and desolate look.

"Are you sure she's in there?" asked Ojo uneasily.

Button-Bright was sure of nothing beyond the inescapable fact that his beloved grandmother had hidden herself away. It hurt him to think this. The little clearing in Gugu Forest was her home. She loved the stillness and the solitude, and she loved sitting in her rocking chair while the sun went down in glory. Dame Zanket had driven her out, if only temporarily.

She might have gone anywhere. Like her grandson Button-Bright, she could use her Yookoohoo powers to transform herself into any form she chose. She might have become an owl, for instance, and holed up in a hollow tree. Or she might have become a catfish and dived to the bottom of a pond. She might even have become a fly, sitting on the roof of the house at this very moment and watching them all unsuspected. But the boys had gotten to know her very well over the past few months, and they knew that she generally spent her nights in a burrow behind her house. She would transform herself into a rabbit, a mole, or some other burrowing creature, make her way down into her dark, winding tunnel, and sleep away the dark hours in peace and comfort. She did not generally go down there by day, however, and if she had done so now it was a very bad sign indeed.

Button-Bright knelt beside the clump of sage. "Grandma Natch! Are you in there? It's us, Grandma Natch. Me and Ojo."

They had always received the warmest possible welcome here. "My boys," Grandma Natch called them, though one was her grandson and one was not. She doted on both of them equally, took extravagant pride in their magic powers, and had perhaps fallen into the grandmotherly habit of petting and indulging them more than she ought. She even welcomed their friends who stopped by, such as Ozma, the lovely girl ruler of Oz, and the famous Wizard. Nothing they did could possibly be wrong. Could it?

Button-Bright called again. Silence reigned.

"She must be somewhere else," said Ojo. "She can definitely take care of herself."

Button-Bright knew this. All the same, he felt more and more strongly that Grandma Natch had gone to ground right here in the privacy of her burrow and that her silence did not bode well. He shouted, "We know about Dame Zanket! We want to help. Please, Grandma Natch!"

A muffled, subterranean "Hmph!" was heard.

"She's there," said Ojo, kneeling beside his best friend. "Grandma Natch!" he called. "It's me, Ojo. Won't you come out and talk to us?"

For a moment nothing happened. They held their breaths. Then there came a sudden scrabbling sound from below, as if something larger and heavier than a rabbit or a mole was heaving itself up through the tunnel. The sound grew louder and an explosion of dirt rattled the sage leaves. When it settled, the boys saw two resentful eyes glaring up at them out of a black and white face with a long, sharp snout. Grandma Natch had never taken the form of a badger before. It did not ease Button-Bright's fears.

"Well?" she growled. A warm welcome, it seemed, would not be forthcoming today.

"We're sorry, Grandma Natch! We didn't ask Dame Zanket to come here. She just showed up."

"Same as all the others? My little house has been quite the destination lately, oh yes it has. There's been a regular parade asking for you!" She had a point. Of all the "clients" so far, only a few had found the boys at the Emerald City. The others had somehow made their way here to Gugu Forest. "I've been as patient as a broody hen," Grandma Natch grumbled. "I put up with that young couple and their squawling baby. I even tried to talk sense to those silly children with their big ideas. But this!"

Her whiskers quivered with outrage. Her black eyes blazed.

"We know," Ojo said shamefacedly. "Dame Zanket is a bit stubborn."

"Stubborn? She's sitting in *my chair!* You'd better get her out of it, because if you don't—well, I might just forget that Yookoohoos mind their own business."

Grandma Natch alluded to a hallowed precept. No right-minded Yookoohoo, she said, would take it upon herself to transform folks who didn't want to be transformed. The short form of this precept was "Mind your own business!" and Grandma Natch observed it faithfully. That she should threaten to turn her back on it now sent chills down Button-Bright's spine.

"We told Dame Zanket we'd take her to Ev," he said quickly.

"Today?"

"Soon. Or rather—well, there's a problem."

"Yeeeeeees?" The word emerged almost as a snarl. Button-Bright hung his head.

"Dame Zanket says she wants us to go on ahead. Without her. To get a place ready."

"I see. And where do you plan to keep her in the meantime?"

Button-Bright writhed. "She says—oh, Grandma Natch! She won't stir a step till it's all settled!"

At this awful announcement, Grandma Natch swarmed the rest of the way out of her burrow and popped up in her true form. The boys had never seen her looking so wrathful, not even when she'd squared off against the fairy Lurline.

Who would wait on Dame Zanket? That's what Grandma Natch wanted to know. Who would feed her, clean her, put her to sleep? Who would cater to her every insane, unreasoning whim? Who would listen to endless extracts from her diary? Not Grandma Natch! They could call Ozma if they wanted to. Or Glinda, or even the little maid Jellia Jamb. But Grandma Natch washed her hands of the whole thing. Grandma Natch would go right back into her burrow and stay there, oh yes she would. Or she might move to some other part of Oz altogether. The Quadling Country must be quiet, now that Dame Zanket had left it.

"But in the meantime," she finished balefully, "nobody, and I mean *nobody*, had better come looking for me till that woman is gone!"

She shrank back down to badger form, still bristling with ire, and whisked out of sight.

Ojo put a sympathetic hand on his best friend's shoulder. "This is terrible," he said.

Button-Bright nodded. He felt as if a wall had fallen on him. "It's our fault. We've got to fix this."

"How? You saw how Dame Zanket was. She won't budge till she's ready. Besides, she wants to die, remember? We can't help her do that, can we?"

"I don't know," sighed Button-Bright. "We definitely can't leave her here."

At that moment, a bloodcurdling shriek was heard.

"Dame Zanket!" both boys said together. They dashed around to the front of the house, fully expecting to see some huge beast crouched over the old lady's prostrate form—or, more likely, cowering from her gimlet glance.

What they saw instead was a small cloud hovering in front of the verandah like an airborne bale of cotton, while the startled faces of Onna Val and Jandilay peered over its feathered edge. At last! Ignoring Dame Zanket, who was madly thumping her cane and shouting about invasions from above, Button-Bright and Ojo made a rush for the cloud.

"Help us up, will you?" they begged over the din. "You won't believe what's been going on around here!"

The facts of the matter were all too obvious to Onna Val. "It seems clear to me," she laughed when they'd poured out their story. "Dame Zanket is a citizen of Oz. That makes it Ozma's problem. Let's go the Emerald City and ask *her*."

Jandilay's pale, worried face lit up at this idea. He and Onna Val currently lived in the Land of An, all the way on the other side of the world, and if matters went well they would soon live in Ev. Yet neither had ever seen the famous Emerald City of Oz and this might be their last chance for a long time to come. Surely they could make a detour on their way.

"Ozma it is," said Button-Bright, grateful to find himself in possession of a plan that, if it worked, would put the whole burden off on someone else. "We'll go right now. Just let me do one last thing." He jumped back down to the ground, collected a handful of pebbles, and spread them out at the furious Dame Zanket's feet.

"Are you trying to bury me?" the old lady shrieked. "I'm not dead yet!"

Paying her no mind, he transformed each pebble into a bowl of bland, lukewarm soup. Then he ran down the steps and clambered back onto the cloud. "South, Onna Val!" he cried! And away they soared.

CHAPTER FOUR

A FESTIVAL FLURRY

ightweight traveling clouds like Onna Val's were
common in far-off An. Long ago a vastly larger version
called Cloudcourt had borne Queen Lurline's whole
entourage around the world, but Onna Val's small cloud
was more than serviceable. It fizzed up out of thin air
whenever she wanted it, and when she'd finished her journey
it disappeared altogether. She steered it with a little
pressure from her hand, at speeds ranging from a leisurely
coast to a breathless rush that left the wind itself gasping.
For Button-Bright and Ojo it made a relaxing change. They
usually did their own flying on wings provided by Yookoohoo
magic.

As they flew, all four friends pondered Dame Zanket's strange request.

"What on earth is that Zanket woman thinking?" cried Onna Val. "Off to Ev at her age. And to do what? Get sick and die? It makes no sense. Now, for Jandilay and me it makes perfect sense. We're young. We want to grow up. Simple enough."

"I wasn't meant to be immortal," said Jandilay. "I was born a mortal boy in a mortal country. I should have grown up and lived a mortal life." They all knew the terrible fate that had overtaken him many centuries ago. He had become a Phanfasm, a spirit of incalculable power, living with his evil fellows on the Mountain Phantastico. Life had become an endless nightmare. Only a chance visit from Button-Bright had given him an opportunity to escape that life and restore his own lost heart.

Onna Val had adopted Jandilay as her special charge and had brought him to live with her in the fairyland of An; indeed, the girl would have done anything to make him happy and comfortable. Yet even there, with work to do and a friend who loved him, he was haunted by nightmare memories and had soon sunk into listlessness. The only thing that roused him was the possibility of seeking a mortal life in Ev.

"Maybe I'm not so different from Dame Zanket," Jandilay sighed. "She's further along than I am, but we both want the same thing."

CHAPTER FOUR

"Huh!" said Onna Val. "We'll see about that." Her vision for their future did not include old age and death. She thought it would be a fine thing if they stayed in Ev for about fifteen years—twenty at the most—and then, in the full splendor of their prime, came back to An or Oz and made an eternal life for themselves. Naturally Jandilay knew nothing of this. It wasn't what he thought he wanted and Onnna Val saw no reason to worry him with it. There would be plenty of time to bring him round when he saw how happy they would be.

As they flew, the purple landscape below gave way to lush green. Ahead lay the Emerald City, glittering in the morning sun. Down glided the cloud until it popped right over the city wall.

Onna Val and Jandilay drank in the view with wonder and delight. A lovely green glow enveloped every boulevard, street, and byway, every plaza, courtyard, and garden. It even enveloped the many green-clad women, men, and children going about their business. Many grand and beautiful public buildings could be seen, and grandest of all was the palace that lifted its spires and domes almost to the sky.

"I've lived in palaces all my life," Onna Val said admiringly. "I've never seen one like this before."

Suddenly Ojo asked, "What's going on by the hen house?"

Below them just then lay the royal gardens, a great walled space filled with lovely trees, fountains, flower beds, and winding paths. On one lawn, outside a small, quaint house, the friends saw a seeming island of bright yellow amid the greenery. This yellow island was not as solid as it appeared; it shifted and jostled like a live thing. Floating up from it they heard a multitude of voices raised in song.

"What is that?" Jandilay wondered. "A garden of singing daffodils?"

Button-Bright laughed. "No, it's just our friend Billina's family. Part of it, anyway. And look, there are the Scarecrow and the Tin Woodman! Let's land there, shall we?"

Soon the four friends stood on solid ground while the traveling cloud fizzed down to nothing at their feet. Onna Val looked excitedly about her. Then she gave a whistle. "Why, they're chickens!" she exclaimed.

She couldn't believe her eyes. The living carpet of yellow comprised dozens of alto and soprano hens, a few tenor and bass roosters, and a contingent of treble chicks, all singing in perfect five-part harmony while following the Tin Woodman's downbeat. Alongside the Woodman stood his great friend the Scarecrow.

On seeing the new arrivals, the Tin Woodman at once lowered his tin baton. The chorus trailed off. Affectionate greetings were exchanged, old friends were embraced, and new friends were introduced.

"Welcome to Oz," the Scarecrow said kindly to Onna Val and Jandilay. "We've heard about both of you and we're delighted to make your acquaintance."

"I believe you helped to save Oz a few months ago," said the Tin Woodman, whose other name was Nick Chopper. "We owe you our thanks."

Onna Val and Jandilay blushed. They had certainly heard a great deal about these two celebrated Oz personages, dear friends and trusted councilors of Ozma and Dorothy, as well as heroes of their own many adventures. It was thrilling to find them as warm and genial as they were extraordinary.

"What's going on?" asked Ojo. "Do you have a concert coming up?"

The Tin Woodman nodded. "Don't you know? Ah, but you've been away. Ozma has declared a festival next week, commemorating our great journey to Ev. It'll be a grand affair."

"Nick and I have composed a chorale for the occasion," said the Scarecrow. "That's what we're rehearsing with the Royal D and D Choir."

"D and D?" asked Jandilay.

"Why, that stands for Dorothy and Daniel!" clucked a feminine voice near their feet.

"Billina!" cried Ojo and Button-Bright, falling to their knees to greet their old friend. And Billina it was, the proud matriarch of all this great brood of chickens. Like Dorothy and the Wizard, the Yellow Hen had come to Oz from the great Outside World and had earned the love and respect of Ozma and her people.

"All my chicks are called Dorothy or Daniel," Billina explained. "It saves trouble."

"Billina will be the top honoree at the festivities," put in the Scarecrow. "In fact, you could say we're only here today because of her."

Onna Val and Jandilay did not know the tale of Ozma's long-ago mission to the Land of Ev. Since they were now going to Ev themselves, however, they begged to hear it from the Scarecrow and Tin Woodman—two of Ozma's companions on that dangerous journey.

It had happened not long after Mad Evoldo threw himself into the sea. Princess Ozma, newly released from an enchantment, had decided to save Evoldo's family from their own enchantment. She had taken a rescue party across the Deadly Desert to Ev—only to fall into the Nome King's clutches herself, along with her friends. They might have remained there still were it not for the cleverness of Dorothy's new friend, the Yellow Hen. Billina had spied out the Nome King's secrets and had broken his enchantments with seeming ease. Moreover, when the furious Nome King had reneged on his promises, Billina's freshly-laid eggs had thrown him into an abject panic. This had allowed Dorothy to capture the Nome King's Magic Belt—again at Billina's insistence—thus depriving him of his best magic and restoring the royal family of Ev.

"What a story!" said Jandilay. "No wonder they're throwing a party for you, Miss Billina."

"Pure luck is all it was," the Yellow Hen clucked. "Anyone else would have done the same." She clearly took great pride in the eminent position her deeds had won her.

"Luck or not," said the Scarecrow, wagging his straw-stuffed finger at her, "you shouldn't be out here. The song we've written is supposed to be a surprise. You mustn't hear it till the day of the celebration."

The Yellow Hen fluffed up her feathers in mock offense. "Well, if I'm not wanted!" She winked merrily at the boys. "By all means carry on. I'm sure I've better things to do elsewhere. As for you children!" Here she addressed her many descendants, still patiently awaiting their cue. "Behave yourselves, stay on pitch, and always watch your conductor." A chorus of good wishes followed her as she stalked away. She clearly commanded her family's respect.

Onna Val had concerns about the story she'd just heard. "This Ev," she said to the Scarecrow and Tin Woodman. "Are you sure it's safe?"

The Scarecrow nodded his stuffed head. "The mad king died long ago, and I'm told that Ev has improved a lot since then. I'm sure you'll get a warm reception."

Button-Bright and Ojo were anxious to find Ozma.

47

"You'll find her in the throne room," said Nick Chopper, "busier than ever."

She was busy indeed. Ozma had taken on decorating chores, and the throne room hummed with activity. There were ladders everywhere (the Patchwork Girl teetered crazily atop one), and bunting and streamers trailed underfoot or waved gaily in the breeze from the open windows. Dorothy, Trot and Betsy were cutting out giant letters which Shaggy Man pasted onto banners. The Wizard was enchanting an elaborate centerpiece. Even the Woozy trotted here and there with tools and supplies on his flat back. As for the little maid Jellia Jamb, she seemed to be everywhere. She would have put Ojo and Button-Bright to work if Ozma hadn't saved them.

"What can I do for you four?" asked the lovely girl ruler.

They explained what had happened at Grandma Natch's house. To their surprise, it turned out that Ozma knew Dame Zanket already.

"Poor Dame Zanket," she sighed.

"What do you mean, Ozma? Where did you meet her?"

"Why, at Flutterbudget Center. You know she's a Flutterbudget?" They didn't. The visitors from An had never even heard of Flutterbudget Center and its unique population. "The town is a haven for people who let their imaginations run away with them," Ozma said. "You might have noticed that Dame Zanket always expects the worst?" They nodded. They could hardly have missed it. "That's

Flutterbudget Center for you. Every so often I try to do something for those poor people. A few can be helped, but not Dame Zanket. Her real problem is simply that she's old. We can't make her any younger. Ever since I've known her she's talked and talked about finding a way to die."

"How unsettling," said the Wizard.

"I agree," replied Ozma. "At first I didn't believe her. Yet the years went by and she never changed. Dame Zanket is nothing if not consistent. Now you tell me this fixation of hers has brought her all the way to the Gillikin Country. Could it be more than just talk?"

"If she ever gets what she wants, I think she'll turn tail and go right back home," Onna Val said stoutly.

"I hope so," smiled Ozma. "But what if she doesn't? What if she truly gives up on life?"

They considered this. Only Jandilay had an answer.

"I think we should respect Dame Zanket's wishes," he said quietly.

Onna Val stared. "You mean we should take her to Ev and leave her there?"

He nodded firmly. "It's her life," he said. "It's her choice."

"And come to think of it," said Button-Bright, "we've done this kind of thing already. I have, anyway."

"What do you mean?" asked the Wizard.

"Why, a woman from Oz died in Ev just last year. That was Comina Dreams, the very first person I ever took there."

"But Comina Dreams was young when she left Oz," Onna Val argued. "That's what you told us. She didn't go looking for death, did she? She wanted to have her baby."

"And she stayed on to live a whole mortal life," said Jandilay. "Including the end."

It was a difficult conundrum. Ozma hesitated. "Perhaps you're right, Jandilay," she said doubtfully. "Perhaps for now we should do as Dame Zanket asks, even though it feels odd to us."

"We can change our minds later," said the Wizard.

"But where in Ev can she go?" Ojo wanted to know. "She can't live by herself. She'll need a lot of care."

"And we need to get her out of Grandma Natch's rocking chair as soon as possible," added Button-Bright. His hopes for a quick solution to this problem were vanishing before his eyes. Poor Grandma Natch!

Ozma said they would have to make inquiries in Ev. "And that brings up another point," she said. "You boys have taken several Ozites to Ev now, haven't you? In a very responsible fashion, of course, and for excellent reasons. Still, Ev is a sovereign nation. It occurs to me that we should have consulted the King first. Or rather, the Queen Regent."

"The Queen Regent?"

"That's right. I keep forgetting. Poor King Evardo fell into an enchanted sleep several years ago. He hasn't woken up since. It's a terrible loss. And it seems that his wife, Queen Fluff—you met her a long time ago, Button-Bright, when she was Princess Fluff of Noland—didn't want to stay on and rule Ev. Ev is ruled now by a woman called Eviret, the eldest of their two daughters. She calls herself the Queen Regent."

"Is she a nice person?" asked Button-Bright.

"I know very little about her," Ozma admitted. "Her father Evardo was an excellent king, so his daughter will probably rule wisely too. I think you should present yourselves at her court and explain the situation to her."

Button-Bright saw no need for this extra step. "We've moved lots of people to Ev," he pointed out. "And we never got permission before."

This was exactly what concerned Ozma, who felt strongly that the Queen Regent should be consulted. "You boys are my ambassadors in this. As representatives of Oz, I trust you to conduct yourselves with diplomacy. Go to the capital city, find the royal palace, and ask to see the Queen Regent. The rest is up to you."

CHAPTER
FIVE

OVER THE
DEADLY DESERT

It was a worried quartet that flew across the Deadly Desert late that afternoon, seated once again on Onna Val's cloud. The noxious fumes drifting up from below did nothing to make them feel better.

At least they knew which direction to fly in. Flying back and forth to Ev had become such a habit that Ojo had recently made Button-Bright sit down with a map and learn something about the place. Ev was a long country, they found, whose southwestern border straddled the northeast corner of the Deadly Desert. On the opposite side of the country lay a long coastline washed by the waves the Nonestic Ocean. At the far north of the map the boys had seen a dot labeled "Red Castle," which meant that it was the home of the Red Jinn—a highly magical person whom they knew from his occasional visits to the Emerald City.

"Are we sure Jinnicky isn't the ruler of Ev?" Button-Bright asked now, as Onna Val struggled to keep them above the Deadly Desert's fumes. Everyone in Oz loved the Red Jinn and Button-Bright thought he would give their request a good hearing.

Ojo said no. "It's funny, though. The royal family of Ev has no magic at all and Jinnicky has lots. Why isn't he king?"

No one knew.

Many miles southeast of the Red Castle, near the exact middle of Ev's coastline, lay a spot marked on the map as "Royal Summer Palace." Dorothy had told the boys that this was where she and Billina had met a horrid person called Princess Langwidere who spent her days trying on an extensive collection of heads. Where most of these heads came from remained unclear, but the imperious Princess had tried to collect Dorothy's and had not liked taking no for an answer. Only Ozma's arrival had foiled her.

Many miles inland from the Royal Summer Palace lay the capital city of Evna, where Ozma had told them they would find Queen Regent Eviret.

Soon they found that they were flying almost directly into the setting sun. "It'll be dark before we get there," said Onna Val. "Maybe when we've passed this awful desert we should stop for the night, and then go on in the morning."

Button-Bright thought of Grandma Natch, holed up in her burrow, angry at the trouble her grandson had brought upon her. He wished they could press on. But Onna Val was right; they would soon lose their way in the dark. Besides, they didn't know what time Queen Regent Eviret went to bed at night. To knock at her door while she slept, he suspected, would not be what Ozma had meant by "diplomacy."

"Diplomacy." What *had* Ozma meant by "diplomacy?" Button-Bright had heard the word before, but it had made no impression on him. He certainly hadn't thought he'd be called upon to exemplify it or embody it in any way. What did it mean? He asked the others.

"Professor Wogglebug hands out diplomas at the College of Athletics," said Ojo. "Maybe that's what diplomacy is."

Onna Val thought not. "It's more like international relations," she said. "A lot of royal families are related to each other, aren't they? For instance, King Evardo married Princess Fluff from Noland. A princess from one country marrying a prince from another country—that's diplomacy."

Button-Bright and Ojo looked at one another in consternation. "We don't want to marry anyone from Ev," said Ojo. "We just want to find a nice place to live for you two and Dame Zanket. Not the *same* place," he added quickly, shuddering as he imagined what it would be like to live with Dame Zanket.

"I don't know," said Onna Val. "Maybe there's another side to this diplomacy business."

"It's beyond me," said Jandilay. "If there's one thing we Phanfasms never, ever worried about, I'm sure it's diplomacy. Well, and charity. You know, our realm was right down at the southern end of Ev. We caused a lot of trouble for the people there. It's strange to think that now I want to live in Ev myself."

"Maybe that's what diplomacy is," suggested Button-Bright. "Making friends with people who used to be your enemies."

"Oz and Ev have always been friends," said Ojo. "No, there has to be more to it than that. I wish we'd asked Ozma when we had the chance."

"We're past the Desert!" cried Onna Val. "Can't you tell? The air is so much better! Come on, let's find someplace to spend the night."

And down they plunged as the sun sank past the horizon.

CHAPTER SIX

A PERFIDIOUS PLOT

There were considerable advantages to traveling with a Yookoohoo enchanter such as Button-Bright. Rather than searching for an uncomfortable shed or barn to sleep in, or prevailing on a disgruntled farmer, the four friends passed a cozy night as rabbits in an abandoned burrow—just the way Grandma Natch might have done. Button-Bright's magic also provided a suitable supper (rather on the bland side, as he freely admitted), so that no one went to bed hungry. As for Ojo, he used his own power to start two fruit trees—peach and apple. By dawn they would be full grown and loaded with delicious fruit.

Ojo and Onna Val woke up first next morning. They detached themselves quietly from the sleek-furred, rabbit-y huddle and made their way above ground.

Gray twilight still enveloped the little wood. The sun had not yet poked its golden head above the horizon and a thin mist drifted among the tree trunks. Fallen twigs and pine needles carpeted the earth under their paws. No picnic basket trees grew here, as they did at the orchards of their Evian friend Darmina. No lunch box or dinner pail trees grew either. These were fir trees, magical only in the most natural sense. Ojo's new trees lifted their loads of fruit far above the two rabbits' heads, which meant that breakfast would have to wait till Button-Bright could restore them all to their natural shapes. Ojo sniffed about near the mouth of their burrow and nibbled a few tender green shoots.

Onna Val watched him dubiously. "How do those taste?"

"Fine just now," said Ojo, who had grown used to this sort of thing. "They won't when we're human again."

"I think I'll wait," said Onna Val. "Thank goodness for your trees! Button-Bright's Yookoohoo food may be handy, but the taste is only so-so. Is that a stream I hear nearby? Elegant! We'll get a nice wash before we leave."

Suddenly she stiffened. She had heard another sound over the chuckle of the stream—harsh voices approaching. Ojo heard them too. In true rabbit fashion, they both froze.

Out of the mist loomed two dark forms. Ojo stared. What was he seeing? Man-like in face and limb, they nevertheless proceeded on all fours across the uneven ground. Why didn't they walk upright? Then Ojo realized: where their hands and feet should have been they sported black, rubbery-looking wheels. By means of these wheels they rolled where they could, or else stepped over rough spots.

Their gorgeously colored, tight-fitting outfits could hardly have been less well-suited to the woodsy environment. Ojo also wondered at the frilly white ruffs the creatures both wore around their necks. He himself had worn such a ruff many years ago and it had never been comfortable. Button-Bright had easily persuaded him to give it up. Why were the creatures dressed this way? Indeed, why were they here at all?

"This is the place," one of them said in a harsh, rasping voice. "It's almost sunrise. We're right on time."

"Let's hope Gando is on time too," the other replied irritably. "And that his spy has given him some real news. I'm tired of waiting for her to act. Does she want to foil the Queen Regent or doesn't she?"

"Oh, don't start!" grumbled the first. "The spy is on our side, all right. But unlike you, Harbo, she's wise enough to wait."

"Wait for what? For all our people to be thrown into prison?"

"For certain possible allies to come around. With the Red Jinn on our side we'd be sure of success."

"The Red Jinn, the Red Jinn. They've been at him for three years and what good has it done? It's as if he doesn't want to finish this thing. I wish we could get hold of King Evardo ourselves. Then we'd find a way to end it once and for all."

"No we wouldn't. Only the Red Jinn can do that."

"Then why doesn't he? Because it's not in his best interests, that's why. Your precious Jinnicky is playing both sides of the fence. He'll never help us, mark my words. And I don't believe our spy will, either."

"Don't say that! Without her we'll get no support at all."

"That's exactly my point! Every time we rely on someone else, we end up disappointed. When will we learn? Only we can defeat the Queen Regent. And the sooner the better."

By this time the eastern sky had brightened and the mist had all but disappeared. As the sun made its first appearance, more wheels were heard close by. The two arguing creatures fell silent, listening. Soon a third wheeled creature rolled out of the trees.

"It's all up!" he said. "Letters have been found. Our spy has gone to the dungeons."

This news was greeted with deep dismay. The spy in question, it seemed, had been so placed that she could gather information within the royal palace itself. In addition, she knew the names and whereabouts of numerous allies within Evna. There would be danger if she talked.

"It's not safe for us here," said one of the wheeled creatures. "We'd better go north."

"I agree, but only as long as it takes to carry out our plan."

"Perhaps. Others will have something to say about that. If we fail, the watch on the city gates will only get worse."

"Well, I don't wish to be enslaved again! Once was enough. And while we wait, the Queen Regent grows stronger every day. Captain Evington is turning the Royal Guard into an army. Soon there will be no hope at all."

"Some say there's no hope now. But the three of us can't decide anything anyway. Come on. We'll meet up with the others and talk things over."

On this the trio agreed. They rolled away among the trees and were lost to view.

The two rabbits stirred for the first time since their quiet had been disturbed.

"What was that about?" asked Ojo. "What were those creatures?"

"Wheelers!" shuddered Onna Val. "Horrid things. I forgot that Ev was where the Wheelers happened. If this is what the Queen Regent has to deal with, I feel sorry for her."

"Why? What do you know about Wheelers?"

Onna Val shook her head. "It's all such a long time ago. Let's wake the others and then I'll tell you about it."

Button-Bright and Jandilay were soon roused. They took an immediate interest in the events they'd missed, and when human forms had been restored, apples and peaches picked and pine cones transformed into omelets and biscuits, they all settled down to listen.

Onna Val came from An, a country which, like Oz, lay under a fairy enchantment of immortality. Indeed, it had been in An that Queen Lurline had broken her first Magic Egg, an act that had changed the world forever. Since then many other countries had been made immortal by the immense power of the Magic Eggs, as well as undergoing strange, unpredictable transformations.

"Ev was a place where bad things happened," Onna Val said darkly. "I was with Lurline. I saw."

No one in Lurline's entourage had seen what the Wheelers were like before the breaking of the Magic Egg, she said, but they certainly saw what the creatures became afterward. "Angry, quarrelsome, ungrateful, and completely impossible. Honestly, you'd think we ruined their lives. The things they said to poor Lurline—why, you wouldn't talk that way to your worst enemy! We got out of there fast. The Wheelers were quarreling when we left and it looks like they're still quarreling now."

"And plotting some kind of rebellion," said Ojo. "How sad for the Queen Regent. First her father, then this."

"Who's this spy the Wheelers talked about?" Button-Bright wanted to know.

"Probably another Wheeler rebel. Those creatures are wicked enough to do just about anything," Onna Val declared. "Believe me."

"Are you sure?" asked Jandilay. "Maybe there's another side to it."

Ojo dismissed this. "Whoever the spy is, they've tried to get the Red Jinn on their side. The Wheelers said so. Jinnicky is a friend of ours, and apparently he's not helping them. That's enough for me. If Jinnicky and Onna Val don't like them, neither do I."

"In that case," said Button-Bright, "we'd better tell the Queen Regent what you heard. And the sooner the better!"

CHAPTER SEVEN

THE CITY OF EVNA

"I'm glad we're not dealing with *that*," said Button-Bright.

In the inconspicuous form of swallows, the four children had landed on the city wall overlooking the great gates. At mid-morning the road in and out of Evna was hopelessly congested. Troops of uniformed guards had a busy time keeping track.

"I don't know," said Onna Val. "People are getting in right enough. It's the ones coming out who run into trouble."

They saw what she meant. Everyone leaving the city was stopped and searched. Carts and wagons, especially, were rooted through and pawed over with extraordinary thoroughness. Even the bottoms of carts were knocked on, pried at, and kicked. What the guards hoped to find never became quite clear. They searched assiduously, however, and only released the frustrated travelers when they'd been fully satisfied.

"Probably something to do with Wheelers," said Onna Val. "Let's get inside and find someplace to transform. Then we can see the place properly." They all agreed, and soon they were walking down the street on their own human legs.

Evna looked nothing like the Emerald City. For one thing, it must have grown up over a period of many centuries for it featured a hodge-podge of architectural styles. More than this, though, its human inhabitants looked less happy and contented than their counterparts in Oz. They hurried along with their faces down, as if they did not quite trust one another. Unhappier still were the Wheelers among them, their sour faces at odds with the white ruffs and bright, tight-fitting garments that distinguished them from the more comfortably dressed citizenry.

"Why do you suppose Wheelers are allowed to live here?" asked Onna Val. "I wouldn't trust them an inch."

"They can't be trusted much," Jandilay pointed out. "Look at the jobs they're doing."

He was right. These Wheelers occupied a niche that might elsewhere have been filled by horses or donkeys. Conveyances of every kind rattled along behind harnessed Wheelers—a team of six for at least one large and rich carriage, pairs of them for smaller and lighter wagons, and even single Wheelers for little one-seaters. Wheeler-drawn rigs represented a small portion of the overall traffic, for most Evites walked on their own legs. But the wealthiest citizens, it appeared, could afford to employ Wheelers in this manner.

An especially large rig ran into trouble when one of its Wheelers tripped over a pothole and lay sprawling in the mud. This threw off his five teammates, all of whom responded with jeers and complaints. The whole affair ground to a halt. As for the coachman, he produced a whip and struck a few blows across the offending creature's back.

"Trying to get yourself fired so you can leave the city?" the coachman shouted. "Dream on. You'll land in prison first. Now get up and pull!"

Button-Bright flinched. "It can't be much fun," the boy said. "Wearing a harness and pulling a carriage full of people. I wonder what the Wheelers think of it?"

"They're probably grateful for the work," said Onna Val. "I don't imagine they're good for much else besides plotting."

"You might plot too, if they treated you that way," said Jandilay.

In other respects the city seemed busy and prosperous. Well-kept houses lined residential streets, and on commercial streets the shop windows offered everything from toys and tools to fashions and furniture.

Turning a corner, the four friends found the royal palace just ahead of them. It was a massive building made entirely of white stone, its walls and towers dazzling in the morning sun. In front of it lay a large plaza where an open-air market plied its morning business. Fruits and vegetables were sold here—and paid for with real money, a thing utterly unknown in Princess Ozma's favored realm. Fresh lunch boxes, dinner pails, and picnic baskets also filled the many stalls and kiosks. Ojo and Button-Bright wondered if any of these had been picked in their friend Darmina's orchards.

"What's going on there?" asked Jandilay, pointing.

A crowd of small children knelt or sat cross-legged in front of a large, gaily painted wooden box that loomed over their heads. A rectangular window had been cut into the near wall of this box and something could be seen moving within it. The four friends drew nearer.

"Why, it's a puppet show!" said Button-Bright. "I haven't seen one since I lived in Philadelphia."

Ojo had never seen a puppet show at all, though he'd heard of at least one puppet troupe in Oz. As for Jandilay and Onna Val, they hadn't known that such things existed. Jandilay was immediately entranced.

"What's it for?" he asked.

"Entertainment," said Button-Bright. "The puppets act out a funny little story and the kids laugh and enjoy themselves."

Indeed, the diminutive audience seemed to find the show hilariously funny. They pointed, shouted, and rocked with laughter while the even more diminutive cast performed its foolish antics.

"How does it work?" Jandilay wanted to know.

Button-Bright tried to remember. "These are called hand puppets. You work them from under the stage. The puppet fits tight over your hand, like a glove, with your fingers inside the arms and head. That's how you make them move."

"They seem so alive," breathed Jandilay.

"That puppet looks like a Wheeler!" Onna Val exclaimed.

It *was* a Wheeler. The little puppet lurched about on all fours, wheels flying every which way in a comical manner. It had an awful temper and shouted outlandish insults at the audience. It also picked up small, soft objects with its front limbs and chucked them at screaming children, a thing no real Wheeler could possibly have done. Onstage with the Wheeler was a blonde lady puppet who simpered and preened and giggled at her companion's bad behavior. She had a magic wand.

"She should give him a good whack with that thing," said Onna Val.

The blonde lady whacked no one, but someone else did after she left the stage. A crowned male puppet beat the Wheeler into submission (not without more insults and abuse) and was rewarded at the end with wild applause. Boos and catcalls greeted the blonde lady's bows. Whoever she was, she seemed highly unpopular. The curtain came down and the audience struggled to its small feet.

"We'd better move along," said Onna Val. "Goodness only knows what the real Wheelers are up to by now."

"No, wait!" begged Jandilay. His eyes shone with excitement. "I have to meet the people under the stage. Don't worry, I'll be right back!" Without waiting for a reply, he ran behind the little theater and disappeared.

Onna Val stared after him. "That was unusual," she said.

"He really liked it," said Ojo. "I couldn't even follow the story."

Neither could Button-Bright. Onna Val thought it simple enough. "A stupid Wheeler misbehaves and the King of Ev puts him in his place. That's all it is. I don't know about the blonde lady, but she's certainly an idiot. And the Wheelers are worse."

"The kids think so too," said Button-Bright. "I didn't much like it myself. The Wheelers are already getting a rough deal around here. Is it right to make fun of them too?"

"It's their own fault," Onna Val insisted. "They get what they deserve."

Jandilay still hadn't come back. At last they went behind the theater and found him deep in conversation with a man and woman dressed all in black. He beckoned to his friends.

"These are the puppeteers!" he told them excitedly. "Vigo and Virra. They do shows all over the city and even out in the countryside."

Vigo and Virra bowed low. "We've never had visitors from Oz," Virra said.

"It's an honor and a privilege," said Vigo.

"Pshaw!" Button-Bright said with a laugh. "We're nobody special."

"Is this the only puppet theater in Ev?" asked Jandilay.

"Oh, no," replied Virra. "We're just one small part of the Royal Puppet Theater of Ev."

"The Royal Puppet Theater of Ev? What's that?"

Puppetry, it seemed, was immensely popular in Ev. Hundreds of puppet plays had been written for performance by companies both small and large, amateur and professional. The largest and most prestigious company was the Royal Puppet Theater of Ev, an enormous operation that boasted two permanent stages, several touring groups, and a large work force.

"From here you can see the top of our main theater," said Vigo, pointing toward a sliver of stone that showed just above the surrounding buildings.

"Who owns the theater?" asked Jandilay.

"The royal family. Our patron used to be Princess Runa, a very smart lady with excellent taste. She knows a good play when she sees one. But now... Well, Queen Regent Eviret runs things and it's nothing but Wheeler farces from dawn to dusk."

"Hush, Vigo!" Virra cautioned. "No one wants to hear about that."

Vigo blushed uncomfortably. "This is just between us, of course," he said. "You'll say nothing? Good. And now I'm afraid we've got a schedule to keep. If you'll excuse us?" The two of them set to work packing their gear onto a cart. Apparently the conversation had ended.

Jandilay bade them goodbye with obvious reluctance. "What an amazing business!" he bubbled when they'd gone. "You can see how much care and skill goes into it. I wonder what the big theaters are like." He speculated about this while they made their way toward the royal palace. None of them had ever seen him quite so excited about anything. He sounded like a normal boy who had never lived the dark and terrible life of a Phanfasm.

He fell silent when they reached the palace steps. Fifty armed guards barred the way.

"Why so many guards?" asked Ojo. "Ozma never has but one."

"Wheeler trouble," said Onna Val.

This seemed possible. The stern faces of the guards did not look friendly. Their priorities, moreover, ran exactly counter to those of their fellows at the city gates. Instead of stopping Evites on their way *out* of the palace, the guards stopped those trying to *enter* the palace. It looked like a great deal of bother.

Button-Bright had an idea. "Why worry these men?" he said. "Let's fly up over the wall and get into the palace that way. Once we're inside we can find the Queen Regent. It'll be a lot less trouble, don't you think?"

"Excellent diplomacy," said Onna Val. "We're saving everyone time and labor while still doing what we meant to do anyway."

It seemed plausible. Besides, all four friends were used to the company of rulers and celebrities. A Queen Regent of Ev couldn't be less welcoming than Queen Lurline of An or Princess Ozma of Oz, could she? In just moments four swallows soared up over the white battlements and back down the other side, where a brief reconnaissance led them to a grassy courtyard filled with trees and flower beds and screened by high walls. No one appeared to be nearby. Button-Bright quickly restored their human forms.

But this last bit of Yookoohoo magic did not go unobserved. There was a shriek, and a terrified maidservant darted out from behind a tree. As she fled indoors, they heard her babbling about spies and sorcerers.

For a moment it seemed laughable. Imagine anyone finding them frightening!

Then they heard the tramp of many feet. The courtyard door burst open. A dozen guards rushed in, their sharp spears leveled at the intruders. Suddenly the whole situation became extremely serious.

It was too much for Ojo. The power of the Magic Egg within him blazed forth, hot and angry. He sprang in front of his friends with his arms outstretched. The guards abruptly lurched to a halt, unable to advance. They appeared to be trapped behind transparent curtains of heat haze—a magic shield that Ojo had placed there with astonishing speed to protect those he loved.

"I am Evington, Captain of Palace Security!" one of the guards shouted. He was a tall, imposing man with a very black moustache, an even blacker beard, and a generous waistline. He wore a sword at his side, and his hat had a large red plume. "In the name of the Queen Regent, I place you all under arrest!"

utton-Bright sighed. All he wanted was a nice, friendly sit-down with the Queen Regent. That would be good diplomacy, wouldn't it? But somehow the cause of diplomacy had not been served. Determined to sort it out properly, he posted himself beside Ojo and said, "See here, why are you pointing spears at us? We've done nothing wrong."

Captain Evington scoffed. "Nothing wrong? You used magic to smuggle yourselves into the Queen Regent's palace! You're using it now to stop us from doing our jobs. Yet you say you've done nothing wrong? I say you're spies for the Wheelers or the traitor Runa—or even for the Red Jinn!"

"That's telling them, Captain!" said one of the other guards.

"We're not anyone's spies," Ojo argued. "In fact, we have information about spies."

"We'll see about that," replied the Captain gruffly. "I arrest you all. Now come with me!"

"What if we don't let you arrest us?" demanded Ojo.

All the guards looked unhappy at this. "But you must!" the Captain protested. "Otherwise we might lose our jobs. Some of us might even be sent to the dungeons."

This did sound dire. Button-Bright wondered who was in more trouble—he and his friends or the guards who were trying to arrest them. He decided to assist as best he could. "I see what you mean, Mr. Captain. Maybe we can help each other. If we let you arrest us, will you take us where we want to go?"

Captain Evington's moustache bristled indignantly. "Never!" he shouted. "I will take you to the Queen Regent!"

The Queen Regent? Ojo nudged his friend. Apparently they were to be hustled off to their exact destination. "Oh dear," said Button-Bright, trying not to laugh. "That's awfully hard on us poor prisoners, Mr. Captain."

"It's meant to be hard," asserted Captain Evington. "Otherwise, why bother?"

"Good point," said Ojo. "Button-Bright, he's got us fair and square."

"I agree. Mr. Captain, you'll have to take us to the Queen Regent, even though that's the last place we'd ever want to go. Now let's get it over with."

"Just don't stick us with spears," warned Ojo. "If you do, we might change our minds."

"Very well," said the Captain, obviously relieved. Even his moustache seemed to relax a little. "Come along, prisoners. The Queen Regent will decide what to do with you."

Ojo lowered his hands. The heat haze of his magic protection faded.

"Good work," Onna Val whispered as the four friends followed their captors into the palace. "The way they do things around here, we might have waited a long time for an appointment. Now we go straight to the head of the line."

They thought they'd be taken to a throne room where the Queen Regent would hear their case. Instead, after a journey down marble corridors and up winding staircases, they arrived at a highly ornate, richly appointed council chamber. A long, heavy table took up most of the room, together with a set of equally heavy chairs, all ingeniously carved and lacquered. Portraits of long-dead kings and queens glared down from the walls. It was a room that sat smugly in its own aura of power and privilege. Low-ranking guards waited outside while Captain Evington ushered his prisoners within.

Around the table sat seven richly dressed men and women whose startled faces turned at once toward the newcomers. A woman seated at the head of the table got up.

"What's this, Uncle Evington?" the woman said. "Who are these children?"

"Invaders, Your Majesty," said the Captain. "Sorcerers. Probably spies from the Red Jinn or the traitor Runa. They entered the palace without permission and fought us with powerful magic. They await your royal judgment."

Queen Regent Eviret surveyed the prisoners. They surveyed her right back. She was a woman of medium height—probably about forty years old, Button-Bright thought—very pretty, with a round face and blue eyes. Reddish-gold hair flowed over her shoulders and a gleaming crown sat on her head. Onna Val couldn't help noticing that her sumptuous gown flattered her well-rounded figure.

"Invaders?" the Queen Regent echoed in a high voice soured just now by annoyance. "Sorcerers? *Spies*? Why, Uncle Evington, your prisoners look like *none* of these things. Yet looks can be deceiving, especially in these *troubled* times. Who knows what's going on in their heads? You say they entered the palace *without permission*?"

Her emphasis caused Evington to fidget uncomfortably. "They did, Your Majesty."

"And *where* was my loyal Captain of Palace Security?"

"Encountering difficulties with magic spells, Your Majesty."

"Oh, Uncle. Magic spells?"

"He's right," Button-Bright spoke up. "All your guards were on duty. We didn't like to worry them, so we flew over the wall. That must have been against the rules, so the Captain arrested us."

"Sorry for any trouble," said Ojo. "We mean no harm."

The Queen Regent held up her pale, red-nailed hand. "One moment," she said. "You say you *flew* over the wall?"

The four friends nodded. "In the form of swallows," said Button-Bright. "Once we got inside I changed us back."

"You see?" interjected Captain Evington. "They *are* sorcerers!"

"Not exactly sorcerers," said Onna Val. "Button-Bright, here, is a Yookoohoo. He does transformations. Ojo is the one who stopped your guards with a barrier spell. They couldn't touch us without his say-so. I fly a nice cloud myself."

"Useful skills," the Queen Regent said thoughtfully. "And the fourth member of your party. What of him?"

"I used to have a few powers," Jandilay said quietly, blushing a little. "But not anymore."

"Interesting. The *only* magic in Ev belongs to the Red Jinn, with whom I am *not* at present on the best of terms. My sleeping father, King Evardo, is in his custody. Tell me the truth, now. Did Jinnicky send you here?"

Ojo was surprised and dismayed to hear this pretty woman speak so of their friend Jinnicky. Nevertheless, he assured her that they knew nothing of enchanted sleepers and that the Red Jinn knew nothing of their mission.

"Then what about my sister, the traitor Runa? Have you been in contact with her?"

"We came on our own, Your Majesty. Button-Bright and I are from the Land of Oz and Onna Val is from the Land of An."

"Oz? An?" The Queen Regent took a step toward them. A hungry look sprang suddenly into her blue eyes. "Then— you are *immortal*?"

Now they were getting somewhere. "That's why we're here," Button-Bright said eagerly. "You see, Onna Val and

Jandilay don't want to be immortal anymore. They want to grow up right here in Ev." There! He'd managed to introduce their real mission.

Eviret's mouth fell open in amazement. She stared hard at Onna Val and Jandilay.

"I don't understand. You two live in the Land of An?" They nodded. "And you are immortal?" They nodded again. "You cannot grow older. You cannot die. Yet you want to settle here—so *that you won't be immortal anymore?*"

"That's it," said Onna Val, much relieved. "You see, Jandilay was born mortal. He was cheated out of his mortal life and he wants it back. I've been wanting to grow up a bit too, though we'll have to see about the mortal life part. Ev is the perfect place for us."

The Queen Regent turned her gaze from Onna Val's face to Jandilay's, then back again. She shook her head in perplexity. "I see no sign of mockery in your eyes," she said at last.

"Mockery? Of course not! We like Ev. We're not mocking anyone."

"No? Yet how else am I to understand your strange words? Who wants to be mortal? *No* one! The whole *world* wants immortality! Yet you come here from the immortal Land of An, young and deathless, for the sole purpose of giving it all *up*? Try to imagine how that sounds to *me*. The Red *Jinn* and his people are immortal. The brutish and depraved *Wheelers* are immortal. Even my Nolander *mother* is immortal. But we, the *real* people of Ev—the royal family itself—we are *denied* the gift of immortality."

Tears trickled down the Queen Regent's cheeks. She seemed almost overcome by the magnitude of her sorrow and hurt.

"That doesn't sound fair," said Onna Val.

"Thank you!" cried Eviret, seizing the girl's hands. "You've understood me perfectly. It *isn't* fair. Why, if you think about it, we're second class *citizens* in our own country. Take my mother, Queen Fluff, for example. On her wedding day she was blessed with immortality by Zixi of Ix! But now, when it should be *my* turn, what do I get? *Nothing!* My mother will be young and pretty forever, while I—*I* already look older than *she* does! The ambassador from Boboland took her for my younger *sister!*"

"Daughter," said Captain Evington. "I'm sure he said daughter."

Eviret gave him a withering look.

"But—wait a moment." Ojo was confused. "Isn't Fluff the sister of Bud, the King of Noland?"

"She is," said Eviret. "Immortal, the pair of them."

"How can that be? I thought Noland was a mortal country."

"Quite so. What a *perceptive* boy you are! You see, it all came about because Zixi *likes* Bud and Fluff. Between you and me, I don't know *why*. They're stuck-up little *busybodies* who look down on the rest of us, though one is my uncle and one is my mother. I'm sure *you* wouldn't care for them. But Zixi gave them both the gift of immortality. She didn't give it to Bud's *people*, did she? The Nolanders live and die as they always did. And she didn't give it to Fluff's *husband*, King Evardo of Ev. Or to *me*, Fluff's own *daughter!*

"And *now* my immortal mother, after *treacherously* taking her helpless husband to the Red Jinn, has *sneaked* back to her immortal brother in Noland—with my sister Runa's help!" More tears appeared in the Queen Regent's eyes. Her makeup began to run. "Can you *believe* it? My mother, my uncle, and my sister, all *plotting* with the Red Jinn and the rebellious Wheelers! Against *me*! And who else might be in league with them? Oh, I wish I knew what the people around me were *thinking*. I should know what *everyone* is thinking *all* the time. It's my *right* as Queen Regent. Anyway, now you understand why I'm a bit *sensitive* about things like immortality and people slipping past my guards. When you have to put your own sister in prison, you stop trusting *anyone*. Please accept my apologies if we've alarmed you."

"There's no need for apologies," said Onna Val.

"We're the ones who should apologize," added Ojo. "We didn't know you were having such a hard time."

"How sweet you all are!" Eviret beamed. "And now we're friends, aren't we? Perhaps we can find a way to help one another."

Button-Bright did not know what to make of the Queen Regent. Though he disapproved of her security measures and resented what she'd said about Jinnicky, he also sympathized with her plight. How would his friends in Oz feel if some had been given immortality and some hadn't? Not too pleased, he thought. Very well, then. Down to business.

He told her about his late friend Comina Dreams, whom he'd brought to Ev so many years ago, and about Comina's daughter and granddaughter and the others who had escaped the immortality of Oz. Ev had been good to them. It still was. Now Button-Bright wished to bring his dear friends Onna Val and Jandilay to Ev, as well as Dame Zanket. Princess Ozma had said they must seek permission from Queen Regent Eviret.

"And don't forget those Wheelers!" Onna Val reminded him when he'd finished.

The Queen Regent gave a start. "Wheelers? Which Wheelers?"

Onna Val told her about the three Wheelers from this morning. Eviret and her uncle listened with gratifying fascination.

"It's just what we guessed," Evington said when he'd heard it all.

"Suspicion has now become fact," said Eviret. "On the other hand, by passing on this information, these foreign visitors have proven themselves people of good will. Children, I'm perfectly *delighted* that you stopped by and we'll *certainly* do our best to make you comfortable."

"Then you'll help us?" Onna Val asked eagerly.

Eviret smiled at her uncle. "We'll give it *very* serious thought," she said. "Meanwhile, you are our royal guests. How can we entertain you? Oh! I have *just* the thing. Tonight the Royal Puppet Theater is giving a performance of *The Fairy Fiasco*. I requested it myself as a special treat to make up for all those boring histories that Runa likes. Runa is *such* a snob. The theater people are *thrilled* to be rid of her at last. You will join me in the royal box."

"A puppet play!" Jandilay was enraptured. "We just saw a puppet play this morning. I loved it!"

Eviret beamed. "Aren't you *sweet!*" she said. "In that case, we'll go to the theater this very *minute*. The play doesn't start for hours, so I'm *sure* dear Halvan will have time to give you a backstage tour. He's the Artistic Director, you know, a *delightful* man who would do *anything* for me. I won't be able to stay myself, as I have *so* much to do. But Halvan will take good care of you. And tonight I'll join you for the performance. Won't that be *nice?*"

They all agreed that it would. Perhaps, in spite of their blunders, this mission would turn out well after all.

"Uncle Evington," Eviret said. "Call Ridj, if you please. He's sure to be close by."

Uncle Evington disappeared. A moment later, to the visitors' surprise, a Wheeler appeared in the doorway. His face wore a bland, blank expression. A pair of small saddlebags had been strapped tightly to his back.

"Oh, Ridj," the Queen Regent said in an imperious tone. "Just call my carriage round, and be quick about it. I'm taking my distinguished guests to the theater. You come along behind with my reticule."

The Wheeler bowed his head and disappeared without a word.

CHAPTER NINE

THE ROYAL PUPPET THEATER OF EV

It had been one thing to see Wheeler-drawn carriages in the streets of Evna. It was something else again to ride in the most magnificent of them all, Queen Regent Eviret's own huge carriage, fitted with all manner of ornamentation outside and every luxury inside. No wonder the six Wheelers harnessed to it wore such resentful expressions.

"The theater's not far," said Button-Bright, eyeing the poor Wheelers sympathetically. "We passed it on the way here. Couldn't we walk?"

"We're taking the carriage," Eviret said grandly. She chivvied the four friends inside, climbed in after them, and drove off. Behind the carriage rolled her Wheeler servant Ridj, his saddle bag now loaded up with his mistress's capacious reticule. It was a brief but unnerving jaunt. Not only were they constantly aware of the Wheelers straining in front of them, but they had to endure the bowing, curtseying, and hat-doffing of human passers-by. The very sight of the royal carriage seemed to throw everyone into frenzies of adulation. Of course this was directed at the Queen Regent rather than at the foreigners; still, no one in the Emerald City behaved like that. They heaved a sigh of relief when they got out at the rear of the Royal Theater.

"When we come back this evening we'll go in at the front," said Eviret. "But today you have the rare *treat* of entering through the stage door. This way, please."

> **ROYAL PUPPET THEATER OF EV**
> **STAGE DOOR**
> **AUTHORIZED PERSONNEL ONLY**

Irrespective of the sign on the door, Eviret swept right in, past a bowing doorman who looked as if he'd worked there for at least fifty years. A bell rang somewhere close by. They proceeded down a drab, dimly lit hall with the Wheeler Ridj at their heels.

"Halvan!" Eviret sang as she tripped along. "It's me, your royal patron. Halvan, dear!"

A door popped open just ahead. In it stood a short, stocky man with a receding hairline and a startled expression on his face. He had a note pad in one hand.

"Your Majesty!" he cried, bowing low. "What a lovely surprise. To what do I owe this great honor?"

"Why, to *me*, of course!" the Queen Regent laughed. "But then, you owe absolutely *everything* to me, don't you? Of course you do. And that's why you'll give these foreign *dignitaries* a tour of the place. Just introduce yourselves, won't you?"

They did so, amid much bowing and hand-shaking. Eviret emphasized more than once that the visitors were here on official business from Oz and An and that they must be treated with due deference. She also fished in her reticule (still strapped to the impassive Ridj's back) and drew out a piece of paper, which she presented to Halvan.

"I'd like to commission a new play," she said. "It's to be about my sister Runa and her *treachery*. You know how popular she's always been? Well, people need to realize how *wrong* they are."

Halvan turned pale. "Are you sure?" he said feebly. "We don't usually do plays about living members of the royal family. And Princess Runa was our patron."

"That's exactly why you *must* do it," Eviret insisted. "She betrayed us *all*. What better revenge than a play that *skewers* her? You won't mind writing it yourself, Halvan. Now remember, you're all dining with me at the palace! Enjoy yourselves!"

And with that she swept out, followed by Ridj.

Halvan's face wore the slightly dazed expression of a man who would rather have been doing something else but must make the best of a bad situation. "Well, now," he said, pulling himself together. "A tour. Where would you like to begin?"

"Wherever you want," said Ojo. "It's all new to us. But sir, I hope we're not putting you out. We know you weren't expecting us, and the Queen Regent . . ."

"Exactly," said Halvan. "The Queen Regent."

"So if you're busy—"

"We're always busy," Halvan admitted. "In the end, though, obliging our royal patron must come first. And truthfully, I enjoy showing off our theater. We take pride in what we do. Now—oh dear, I hope you won't be offended. I have a small favor to ask. Would you mind if my assistant comes with us?"

Unnoticed till now, a Wheeler had rolled silently out of Halvan's office. The creature stood stock still, watching them.

"This is Drax Mongo," Halvan said. "He won't be a bother, I promise. Very humble, very discreet. And he does know his theater history. If you have any questions that I can't answer, perhaps Drax can." This eminently reasonable suggestion did not seem to require an answer. Halvan waited expectantly, however, and as the silence lengthened his smile slowly faded. "Or Drax can stay behind!" he added, wringing his hands. "I wouldn't want to make anyone uncomfortable."

Button-Bright caught on at last. "Are you asking our permission? For goodness sake, it's your tour. Of course Drax can come."

"Especially if he knows theater history!" Jandilay said eagerly.

Halvan heaved a sigh of relief and wiped a line of sweat from his brow. "Let's start across the street at the Shop," he said. "Just follow me." He led them back out through the stage door, followed by the silent Drax.

The Shop, as Halvan called it, turned out to be an immense warren of workshops occupying an entire city block. There were workshops where finished wood was carved and shaped into furniture, props, and marionette bodies. Smells of sawdust and varnish filled the air. There was a paint workshop, where artisans mixed the colors that would be applied to wooden faces and set pieces. In the scenic workshop the visitors had to step around a partially painted backdrop spread out across the floor. Jandilay peered at the handiwork of the three paint-splashed artists who bent over it with brushes in hand.

"It looks like an underground cavern," he said.

"For a new play about the Nome King," Halvan informed him. "Nome King stories have been very popular over the years."

"Not with the Queen Regent," said the Wheeler Drax.

Halvan squirmed. "No," he said. "Her tastes are . . . different. This way, please!"

Next they went to the costume shop, where workers produced jackets, pants, tunics, gowns, skirts, blouses, coats, shoes, and anything else that might be worn by a marionette character. Many finished puppets could be seen, representing a wide variety of types and personalities. Jandilay had questions about all of it, and while Halvan did his best with these, he often deferred to Drax Mongo. The reason soon became clear: Drax was found to possess an encyclopedic knowledge concerning every aspect of the theater. There was nothing he didn't know about it. Soon Jandilay directed all his questions to the Wheeler, who seemed to appreciate his interest and enthusiasm.

"You'll let this be our secret, won't you?" Halvan said nervously. "The Queen Regent doesn't need to know."

After a wig workshop they were shown a large and complicated electric board.

"Stage lighting," Halvan said. "Big improvement there, as Drax will tell you. We didn't have electricity when he started out."

"And when was that?" asked Onna Val.

Drax and Halvan looked at each other. Halvan hesitated, then gave a little nod.

"Almost two hundred years ago," Drax said quietly.

Onna Val gaped. "Two hundred years? But that means you're—"

"Immortal. Yes, Wheelers are immortal."

"And humans aren't. So that's what the Queen Regent is so upset about! I'd be mad too."

Drax pressed his lips together as if he were holding back a retort.

"Now, now!" interjected Halvan, becoming a little flustered. "No need to go into all that. Look, the workers are putting down their tools and heading to lunch. Perhaps you'll join us in the cafeteria?"

All the workers ate lunch in a communal cafeteria, it turned out. At first they seemed to keep their distance from the four friends, perhaps even to regard them with suspicion. Jandilay's new-found volubility broke the ice, however, and soon everyone relaxed and got to know each other. Button-Bright was asked to demonstrate his Yookoohoo powers, while Ojo managed to grow a small beanstalk out of his bean stew. Onna Val conjured up her traveling cloud and gave rides on it. As for Jandilay, he wanted to meet everyone and soon took to table-hopping with an enormous grin on his face.

"He's a different person here," Onna Val whispered to Ojo. "It's wonderful! The Queen Regent just has to let us stay. I wonder if Halvan would give him a job?"

Wheelers served as waiters of a sort. They collected trays of food from the kitchen and carried them on their backs to the hungry laborers. Both Wheelers and humans, Button-Bright thought, appeared so uncomfortable with this arrangement that more than one worker whispered a quick apology to his irritable-looking server.

After lunch they visited the stage. Jandilay could not get over the wonders he beheld: the fly space soaring over their heads, the catwalks where the puppeteers did their work, the props and bits of scenery leaning against the far wall, and a small desk where the stage manager ran shows. Jandilay's eyes grew bigger and brighter with every passing moment. "I never want to leave," he kept saying.

There was a small orchestra pit in front of the stage, and musicians had begun assembling in it. Halvan beat a hasty retreat.

"We'd better leave them to it," he whispered. "I'll be scolded if we disturb a rehearsal."

"Do all the productions have music?" asked Ojo.

"Some have a great deal of music," said Drax Mongo. "Songs play a big role in the puppet theater, and singers and voice actors are highly prized." He seemed about to continue, but he thought better of it and left the subject there. They made their way out into the theater lobby.

"Why, here's a bookshop!" said Jandilay.

Indeed there was, a large bookshop containing an astonishing array of books. Drax explained that most of these were plays that had been written especially for the puppet theater. "Our art form is hundreds of years old," he said. "And there have been great playwrights in every age. Take a look."

"Here's a section of Nome King plays," said Button-Bright, indicating one fat shelf.

"And here's a section of Oz plays," said Ojo. "*The Lovelorn Lady of Oz, The Magic Dishpan of Oz, The* Crescent Moon *of Oz*. Oh, and *The Yellow Hen of Oz*. That must be about Billina! I'd love to see it."

"Billina is a favorite character," said Drax. "Or rather, she was. She's a little out of favor at the moment. All the Oz plays are."

"Why is that?"

Before this question could be answered, Halvan chimed in. "Tastes change. What's popular one season will be forgotten the next. What can we do? These days we spend our time on Wheeler farces that no one cared about just four years ago. They're not what you'd call high art, but the Queen Regent adores them. You'll see one tonight. And now I'm afraid Drax and I are due at a rehearsal. Where can I leave you while you wait for your hostess? Ah, I know the perfect spot!"

The four friends soon found themselves in a studio with a piano, a piano player, and a Wheeler who introduced himself as the vocal coach.

"Give them a beginning voice lesson," Halvan said to the Wheeler. "They'll love it."

And that is exactly what happened.

CHAPTER
TEN

IN THE
ROYAL BOX

The day had been a momentous one for Jandilay, but what finally sealed his fate was that evening's performance.

"If you please, Your Majesty, I'd rather not sit in the Royal Box," he announced over dinner, astonishing everyone. Eviret suspected him of ingratitude. Onna Val suspected him of feeling unwell. Captain Evington suspected him of dark designs. All became clear, though, when he explained that his dearest wish was to pull up a chair alongside the stage manager's desk and watch the entire show from backstage. If the request seemed a tad unorthodox, it was nonetheless easily granted—especially since Halvan turned out to be the stage manager that night.

"And I suppose *you* want to join the choir," Halvan added to Onna Val.

This was no joke. Onna Val had created a stir of her own up in the vocal studio. While the others struggled with the most basic warm-up exercises, she had filled the room with a warm, effortless, penetrating alto that seemed to come out of nowhere. If it had startled Onna Val herself, it had electrified the Wheeler vocal coach. At first he had taken it as an affront to his professionalism. Exercise after exercise he had given her, each more difficult than the last, apparently in the hope of tripping her up. She had mastered even the thorniest rhythms and landed right on the note every time.

"I don't see what you're all so fussed about," she had said finally. "It's not that hard."

The vocal coach thought otherwise. After satisfying himself that Onna Val's gift was real, he had declared that he would speak to Halvan about it. He must have Onna Val in his choir. She glowed.

She couldn't start work yet, though, and that evening she happily took her seat with the others in the Royal Box.

The auditorium was built in the shape of a horseshoe, with the stage and orchestra pit at one end, two tiers of boxes at the other, and the rest of the audience seated between. The Royal Box dominated the center of the first tier, open on three sides and a little forward of the other boxes so that anyone sitting in it could be seen by as many people as possible. This allowed the Queen Regent to chat with acquaintances in the neighboring boxes.

"*The Fairy Fiasco*," read Button-Bright from the printed program. "What's a fiasco?"

"I think it's something that goes terribly, horribly wrong," said Onna Val. "Or no, wait—is it some kind of party?"

"Maybe it's a really horrible party," suggested Ojo. He did not much care for parties of any kind and even now felt ill at ease in this mercilessly public, highly exposed location. Audience members were constantly turning around to see who'd been invited into the Royal Box. Ojo could not stop blushing.

Button-Bright never much minded where he was. "Look at the list of characters," he said. "There's somebody here called Lurline. You don't suppose it's our own Lurline, do you?"

Onna Val flipped through the pages. "I don't know," she said. "There's nothing here about the story."

"Would you want to see a play about Lurline?" Ojo asked her. Lurline and her brother Jinjin were the rulers of Onna Val's home country, the Land of An, and two of the most celebrated and honored fairies in the world. Onna Val had known both of them for over three hundred years.

"Maybe. I suppose it depends on what kind of play it is."

Ojo frowned. If the word "fiasco" did indeed mean something that goes horribly wrong, then the *The Fairy*

Fiasco might not flatter Lurline. They would find out soon enough. The lights were going down and the Queen Regent was taking her seat.

"Isn't this a *thrill?*" she whispered. "Your *first* puppet play. Oh, I *do* hope you like it!"

They certainly enjoyed the overture. One toe-tapping tune followed another, and the catchiest tune returned for a rousing climax. Onna Val showed off by humming along. Eviret shushed her.

The curtain rose to reveal a lawn in front of a palace. A handsome marionette man and his well-dressed wife sang a song indicating that they were the king and queen of Ev, that the palace was their country home, and that they must soon return to Evna. At the end of the song they called their servants together.

These marionette servants, when they arrived, caught Button-Bright's attention. He nudged Ojo. "They're dressed just like Wheelers!" he whispered. Eviret shushed him. Ojo nodded, noting the now-familiar garish, tight-fitting clothes and white ruffs. Yet the servants were not Wheelers. They were perfectly ordinary men who walked upright and bowed respectfully to their royal masters.

The second musical number was an ensemble during which the royal couple gave instructions and the servants promised to behave themselves during their masters' absence. But as soon as the king departed, the servants showed their true natures.

First they sang a crude song that abused and insulted the royal family. Throughout this song, one servant after another dashed into the palace and returned wearing wheeled shoes. When all had been thus equipped, they fell to carrying on and whizzing about in the most disgraceful fashion. This sequence, in addition to revealing the bad manners of the servants, also showed off the skill and dexterity of the unseen puppeteers, who managed their impossible choreography so seamlessly that they earned a round of applause from the audience. The shameless servants then threatened still worse outrages, bragging about the money and valuables they would embezzle or steal and the food and wine they would gulp down. A stupider and wickeder lot could hardly be imagined. Onna Val joined freely in the audience's laughter.

At the height of the revelry, a very different figure floated magically down out of the sky. This was a short, plump, blonde lady with a wand and a flock of small winged fairies.

Ojo nudged Button-Bright. "She looks just like the silly puppet lady from this morning," he whispered. "You don't think...?"

Eviret shushed him. But as Ojo had feared, the ridiculous blonde lady's song introduced her as Queen Lurline and conveyed her desire to bless them all with a sublime enchantment. The audience roared at this. In an insufferably squeaky voice punctuated by giggles, the lady sang:

I know a little spell,

A sweet little spell,

And I know it quite as well as ding-dong, ding-dong bell!

You'll treasure it, I know,

From head to tippy-toe,

You'll treasure it with ha-ha, ho-ho-hoooooo!

On the final *ho* she waved her wand. The spell was cast. All the servants spun out of sight in a whirl of strings and ruffs. Lurline waved her wand a second time and the servants returned—as full-fledged Wheelers.

There followed a bizarre number during which the Wheelers cursed Lurline for what she'd done to them while she obtusely took all their grumblings for gratitude and admiration. The more they complained, the more she preened and giggled. The audience couldn't stop laughing. Onna Val's laughter had dried up. Lurline sang:

I'm so cunning, I'm so clever!

No, don't thank me now or ever.

All of us will live forever!

Immortal you, immortal me, immortal we

Will snub the royal familee,

With a tra-la-la, hoo-hoo, hee-hee!

The curtain came down. Act I was over.

CHAPTER ELEVEN

AN INCENDIARY INTERMISSION

"Oh, it makes my blood *boil!*" fumed Eviret. "That *silly* fairy and her *silly* wand. She botched the whole *thing*. I wish she was here *right now*. I'd give *her* a piece of my mind."

Onna Val said, "Your Majesty, it wasn't like that."

Eviret gave a start. "What wasn't like what, dear?"

"*It.* Our time in Ev. It wasn't like that. *Lurline* wasn't like that."

Red spots appeared in Eviret's cheeks. "You mean the play? However would *you* know?"

"I know!" said Onna Val.

"But it happened more than two hundred *years* ago, right here in *Ev*. You can *read* about it in our twenty-two volume history of Ev. I'll lend you my copy."

"I don't need to read your histories," said Onna Val. Her tone was resolute, though she did not raise her voice. "I was *here*. I saw it all."

"Don't be silly. You're only a girl."

"An immortal girl. A three-hundred-year-old girl. Your Majesty, I lived with Lurline on Cloudcourt. I went with her to all those countries. I watched the breaking of all those Magic Eggs. And even though it was two centuries ago, I remember everything."

Eviret seemed rooted to the spot. Her mouth hung open and her eyes were as round as blue moons. But she soon recovered her faculties. She turned to the boys.

"Oh, you immortals and your *funny* ways! I never *know* when you're pulling my leg. Your friend can't *possibly* mean what she says, can she?"

"I believe she does," said Button-Bright.

"Of course she does," said Ojo. "I saw her on Cloudcourt myself."

"*You*? But—are you three hundred years old too?"

Ojo assured her that he was not. He and Button-Bright had journeyed back through time, he said, to the day when Lurline transformed Oz into a fairyland. It was then that Ojo had visited the fairy queen on Cloudcourt and met

Onna Val. Until tonight he hadn't specifically considered the likelihood that Onna Val had also witnessed the transformation of Ev, but it made perfect sense that she would have.

"That's right," said Onna Val. "And Your Majesty, it wasn't at all like your play."

"Indeed? *Just* what was it like?"

"For one thing, Lurline isn't fat and silly. She's beautiful and good. It's true she's made some mistakes—so would you if you'd lived for a thousand years. But she's not stupid, like the Lurline in your play. And another thing! She never did magic with a wand. Some fairies do, but not Lurline. No wand ever made a fairyland."

"That is absolutely false!" declared Eviret. "All authorities agree she had a magic wand. How else did she cast her spell on Ev?"

"It wasn't a spell!" Onna Val retorted. "It was a Magic Egg."

"A *what*?"

This was clearly new territory for the Queen Regent. Onna Val explained as patiently as she could that, as far as she knew, an ordinary country could only be transformed into a fairyland through the power of a Magic Egg. And Magic Eggs were laid only by the Phoenix, an ancient bird that lived high in a remote mountain region of An. The Magic Eggs of the Phoenix never hatched. Filled with the concentrated essence of fairy power, they simply piled up over the centuries. Lurline had made the long and arduous journey to the Phoenix's nest and had taken as many Eggs as she could carry. Then she had traveled around the world on Cloudcourt, breaking Magic Eggs and transforming mortal countries into immortal fairylands.

"None of that comes into *our* histories," Eviret sniffed. "Why should it? Lurline's doings elsewhere are *no* concern of ours. But I do know this: your queen must have made *scrambled* eggs here in Ev, because everything that she did went *wrong*."

"Like what?"

"Everything! All her magic went up into the *north* of Ev, where the Red Jinn lives. And *he* had his own magic already! So he just got *more* magic—and immortality as well! No one can *touch* him now. The rulers of Ev don't rule *him*. Down here in the middle of Ev, where all the *real* people live, we didn't get any magic at all. *None!* No magic, no immortality, *nothing*. We were *cheated*! Oh, except for the *Wheelers*. They had the Summer Palace all to themselves, just as it says in the play, and the magic hit *them* all right. The stupidest, meanest, greediest creatures in Ev became immortal. But the royal family of Ev? Mortal, mortal, mortal! Your queen has a *lot* to answer for, my dear!"

Onna Val had no ready answer. She had imagined that Lurline must be revered in all the countries where Magic Eggs had been broken. To find out that this was not the case in Ev, that in fact the Evites viewed Lurline as a bungling nitwit, horrified and saddened her. The silly blonde lady in this morning's puppet show—that's what the Evites thought Lurline was. Could they have a legitimate grievance? Onna Val herself had admitted that the Wheelers were a mistake. Had other mistakes been made?

While she hesitated, Ojo took up the cause. "You should be glad it wasn't worse," he told Eviret. "Magic Eggs are very unpredictable. I should know. I swallowed one."

She gazed at him in fresh amazement. "You *swallowed* a Magic Egg?"

"Yes, in a way. Lurline had baked it into a loaf. Someone stole it, and—well, it was an accident. But the magic is still in me. And I can tell you, it's not a comfortable feeling."

Eviret didn't care how uncomfortable it might be. "Is that how you held off my uncle's men this morning? He said you had powerful magic, but I didn't believe him. He is far too ready to blame anyone except himself when things go wrong."

Ojo apologetically confirmed Evington's story. Questioned further, he told Eviret still more about his unusual powers—how they slept within him until danger forced him to protect his friends. No, he had not yet tried them on large forces such as armies. He hoped he never would. And no, his powers almost never came up short. Only the mighty Jinjin had ever overmastered him.

As the lights dimmed for Act II, Eviret returned to the subject of Lurline's misdeeds. "So these wonderful Magic Eggs are handed out to Jinns, Wheelers, and little *boys*, but *not* to the royal family of Ev. Onna Val, your fairy queen *failed* us. We were *cheated*! Get us a new Magic Egg of our very own and *then* we might have something to talk about."

None of them enjoyed the rest of the play. Had the Queen of An wronged the people of Ev, Onna Val wondered? Did the Evites deserve some form of reparation? And in addition to all that there was still Jandilay, who had clearly fallen in love with the puppet theater. It had seemed possible that both he and Onna Val might find a home here. Had she spoiled their chances by alienating the company's royal patron? If so, she would never forgive herself.

Button-Bright was remembering his own time-travel adventures and his very first meeting with Grandma Natch, who had taken umbrage at Queen Lurline's magical meddling. Button-Bright had sympathized. Who was this fairy queen to break powerful, world-changing Magic Eggs wherever she pleased? What gave her the right? Had she consulted anyone in Ev or Oz before she did it? True, all had turned out for the best in Oz, as even Grandma Natch grudgingly admitted nowadays. But in Ev? Perhaps not. And what about Button-Bright's mission on behalf of Grandma Natch and Dame Zanket? Had that been ruined?

After the final curtain, it was a quiet group that made its way from the Royal Box to the stage door. The Queen Regent's face was a dark cloud promising inclement weather.

By contrast, Jandilay emerged from the stage door exhausted and happy. Halvan had indeed invited him to stay on as a production assistant. Onna Val could join the choir. Both would live with the other artists here in the theater, where they would learn the ways of the stage. Halvan wanted to know how soon they could move in and start working.

"That remains to be seen," said Eviret.

"What do you mean?" Halvan asked. "I thought Your Majesty would favor the plan."

"I might," she said. She spoke in an uncharacteristically clipped tone, without her usual extravagant emphases. "And then again I might not. I've been giving the matter some thought, and there are two conditions that must be met before we proceed."

"I don't understand. What conditions?"

Eviret turned her blue eyes upon Onna Val. "You say the gift of immortality comes from Magic Eggs, and these Magic Eggs can be baked into loaves? Very well, then. If a ninny like Lurline can bake immortality, so can I. Condition Number One: get me a Magic Egg!"

The girl stared back at her. "A Magic Egg? I don't know if I can do that."

"Find a way! Next, let's return for a moment to the subject of my enchanted father. King Evardo is being held by the Red Jinn. With a Magic Egg of my own, naturally, I can go to Jinnicky myself and force him to give my father back. But what if Onna Val fails to get an Egg? I'll be as helpless as I am now. Condition Number Two: Ojo and Button-Bright, you must go to the Red Castle at once, seize my father, and return him to me."

The two boys gaped. Jinnicky was their friend and a highly powerful magician. What if he didn't want to part with the unconscious king?

"Insist," purred Eviret. "Besides, I'll probably be right behind you with my own Magic Egg. And if you do not succeed—why, there *might* be unpleasant repercussions. Your immigrant friends from Oz, for instance—the ones who already live here. They would have to be sent back where they came from."

Sent back where they came from? All the boys' friends?

"It would be *awful*, to be sure," Eviret admitted. "Where would the poor things *go*? No, it would be *much* better if we found a way to keep them here, along with Onna Val and Jandilay. I'm *sure* we can do that—if only you children meet these two small conditions I've made.

"You'll want to set out in the morning—all except Jandilay, of course. He'll remain here as my *guest*. The others will see him again when you return. So: a Magic Egg and my father. Those are my conditions. Agreed? Back to the palace we go!"

With a satisfied smile on her face, the Queen Regent led the astonished friends back to her carriage.

CHAPTER TWELVE

JANDILAY ENTANGLED

f Onna Val went to bed that night in a state of shock, she woke up next morning in one of grim determination.

"Eviret is right," she told Jandilay on the small balcony that adjoined her room. "Lurline owes this country a Magic Egg. She made a big mess here in Ev, even if she didn't do it on purpose, and this is her chance to clean it up."

"She won't like it," Jandilay predicted worriedly.

"She'd better like it!" retorted Onna Val. "Besides, she owes you too. Never fear, Jandilay. I'll get that Magic Egg if it's the last thing I do. Wish me luck!"

And without waiting for an answer, she whipped up her traveling cloud and zoomed off over the palace wall.

CHAPTER TWELVE

It wasn't long before Ojo and Button-Bright flew after her, setting out on their own quest. They looked a great deal less sure of themselves, even in swallow form, than Onna Val did—and less sure of Eviret, too. At least that's what Jandilay thought. But away they went just the same.

Jandilay was left alone.

He drifted back indoors and considered his position. That he was being held as surety seemed clear. It almost made him laugh. In his Phanfasm days no chains or walls could have held him, for Eviret and all her people would have been at his mercy. But since then he had willingly become an ordinary young man of no special ability who, while he heartily disliked the Queen Regent, nevertheless saw that pleasing her was the best way to establish himself at the Royal Theater.

At the same time, he was not under guard. Why shouldn't he go where he pleased within the city? He decided to find out. If he made it as far as the theater, his lot might not seem so dire.

He remembered the way out of the palace and walked it calmly and deliberately. Nobody recognized him or noticed him. It was only when he approached the gates that he saw someone he knew—Ridj, the Queen Regent's Wheeler aide. Ridj hailed him and rolled forward with an obsequious bob of his dark head, almost as if he'd been waiting there for that purpose.

"Good morning, young master. Please allow me to extend my congratulations. The Queen Regent tells me you'll be our guest for some days."

If the Wheeler meant any of this ironically, it didn't show in his face.

"Thank you," said Jandilay. "It's an honor."

"Doubtless. And while you're here you're free to do as you like and go where you please. Our ruler only wishes that you dine with her each evening and sleep in the room she has given you. May I tell her that this is agreeable?" Jandilay said it was. "Most kind. You're on your way to the theater?"

How had Ridj guessed? He was the queen's own aide, of course, and even as a member of a despised class he must know a great deal about her business. Had he been sent to spy on the foreigner? "That's right," said Jandilay. "I want to talk to Halvan about working there."

"Ah, Halvan," said Ridj. "What luck. Our ruler gave me a scroll for him. It's in my saddle bag. If you wouldn't mind taking it with you? Excellent. And I myself have a message for Halvan's assistant. Perhaps you met him—a Wheeler, like me?"

"Oh! Drax Mongo. Do you know him?"

"My last name is Mongo too," Ridj answered blandly. "Drax is my brother."

Stranger and stranger. Jandilay hadn't stopped to think that Wheelers could have families, but of course they must. "I'll gladly take your message," he said. "What shall I tell Drax?"

"Two things. First, a power surge is expected and the tour must begin at once. Second, there are no aphids on the plant. Can you remember that?"

Jandilay repeated the odd messages back. Ridj appeared satisfied and ushered him out through the gates, instructing the guards to let him come and go as often as he liked. Jandilay hurried off in a state of utter perplexity.

What did the messages mean? Was he being spied upon? Was he being asked to spy on Halvan? Or both?

Perhaps it didn't matter, since anyone spying on him would have a dull time of it. What mischief could he possibly get up to? As for the theater people, they seemed wholly absorbed in their work. If Jandilay were of a mind to report nefarious doings, he would have to invent them. And what would they be? He had no idea what the Queen Regent feared or suspected—at least here in Evna. There was someone called the Red Jinn that she didn't like, but that had nothing do with the theater. And she clearly had issues with the Wheelers, though she trusted one of them enough to keep him with her at all times. No, the whole thing baffled Jandilay. He would be better off saying nothing at all.

He found Halvan in his office with Drax Mongo.

"Good morning, my lad!" the director greeted him. "Ready to start, eh? Good, good. What have you got there?"

"A letter from the Queen Regent," said Jandilay, presenting the scroll. "Ridj Mongo gave it to me. He also gave me messages for you, Drax. I can't make heads or tails of them myself." Jandilay repeated the nonsensical messages to Drax. A momentary look of alarm seemed to flicker across the Wheeler's ordinarily bland features, then vanished. "I hope it's not bad news," Jandilay said.

Drax bowed his head. "Our ruler would not say so," he replied. "Please don't give it another thought."

Halvan found his scroll even more worrisome. He showed it to Drax, read it again himself, folded it into a tight

little square and put it in his pocket. For a moment he seemed at a loss. Then he squared his shoulders and attempted a cheerful smile.

"Very well, lad," he said. "Today your job is to follow us wherever we go, listen to everything we say, observe everything we do, and generally learn whatever you can. In due course we'll start giving you work of your own. It will be very simple work at first, perhaps even tedious. If you do it patiently and well, it will get harder. All clear? On we go!"

And go they did! The day began with a production meeting, during which department heads examined set and costume designs for Drax's approval. It continued up in the music studio, where a team of songwriters presented new songs—again, to Drax. Back in Halvan's office there was an edited program to be okayed by Drax. A hasty lunch followed, and then a rehearsal onstage. Jandilay drank it up avidly.

At the same time, he noticed that Halvan's worried expression never quite disappeared. As for Drax, his usual equanimity grew more and more frayed. Though he was running the rehearsal, he seemed distracted at best and irritable at worst. At last he snapped.

"I can't do this anymore!" the Wheeler erupted, startling the puppeteers. "I shall go mad! Jandilay and Halvan, please come to the office. Now!"

CHAPTER
THIRTEEN

DRAX MONGO'S
TALE

They went to the office. A sweating Halvan closed the door behind them.

"Show Jandilay the letter!" Drax barked.

"Are you sure that's wise?" asked Halvan.

"No!" shouted Drax. "But what else is to be done? I can't work this way!"

This is what Jandilay read:

> *My dear Halvan,*
> *It has come to my attention that your new apprentice, Jandilay, is or was a Phanfasm.*
> *He and his friends claim that he has renounced his powers, but I need not tell you how important it is that we keep watch on him. You will be my eyes and ears in this.*
> *He may even be a spy of the Red Jinn's. Keep me apprised of his words and actions.*
> *Your Royal Patron,*
> *Queen Regent Eviret*

"Well?" said Halvan.

Jandilay took a deep breath. Everything seemed to have changed. All day it had become increasingly clear that Halvan did not in fact run the Royal Theater. Drax did. Drax understood the place from top to bottom and had the respect of its whole staff, while Halvan was merely an assistant—a highly valued assistant, perhaps, but an assistant nonetheless. He and everyone else answered to Drax. Yesterday's tour had been a charade intended to deceive the Queen Regent and her friends. Why had the mask been dropped now and how would it affect the new recruit's future? Jandilay knew only that he must answer all questions as truthfully as he could.

"I used to be a Phanfasm," he admitted. "I lived on the Mountain Phantastico for centuries. I had terrible powers. My heart was maimed inside me."

Halvan sat down and put his head in his hands.

"I know how this must sound," Jandilay continued hopelessly.

"Do you?" demanded Drax. "Young man, the south of Ev is deserted. Deserted! Has been for time out of mind. No one can live within a hundred miles of the southern border. Why? Because there are Phanfasms on the other side! And now you tell me we've hired a Phanfasm into our company, the company we're responsible for!"

"Now, Drax," said Halvan. "Consider the source. Eviret's letter was clearly meant to alarm us, but doesn't it also say this young fellow has lost his powers? Perhaps we should find out what that means."

Drax scowled. "Maybe, maybe. Very well. Jandilay, what does it mean?"

Jandilay told his story: how he had been born a mortal; how he had been tempted to become a Phanfasm; how he had lived on their mountain for many long, lonely years, paralyzed by his own destructive power; how Button-Bright had first befriended him and then, miraculously, had given him the means to free himself from his ancient curse. "I'm not a Phanfasm anymore," he finished. "I couldn't work magic if I wanted to. But I don't want to. All I want is to live a mortal life. I'll live it here if you let me. If you don't—well, I understand."

Drax weighed this. For a moment or two he rolled up and down the room, just as a man with two working feet might pace. "Halvan," he said finally. "What does the Queen Regent want? She wants to pit us against one another! Divide and conquer, as the saying goes. But I say it's *she* that doesn't trust this young fellow Jandilay."

"She doesn't trust us, either," said Halvan. "Perhaps then we *should* trust one another?"

"Exactly. Why would she place a spy among us and then make sure he's not welcome? She wouldn't. My brother's private message only confirms this: '*There are no aphids on the plant,*' he said. "

"I didn't understand that at all," said Jandilay.

"You weren't meant to. It was Ridj's way of telling me to trust you. And I believe I will."

Jandilay thanked him from the bottom of his heart. "I thought there was something fishy about all this," he said. "And then that play last night, *The Fairy Fiasco*. That isn't how the Wheelers came to be, is it? It's all lies, isn't it?"

"Lies dressed up in a few sad rags of truth. Shall I tell you how it really happened?"

Jandilay nodded earnestly. Drax began.

Before Lurline came, he said, the Wheelers were fully human. *The Fairy Fiasco* had at least gotten this right. Many were servants in the Summer Palace, where Ridj Mongo supervised; others worked under Drax Mongo at the nearby Royal Summer Theater, the largest theater outside Evna. Both palace and theater employed men only, servants of the crown and slaves in all but name. They were forced to wear white ruffs and bright-colored, tight-fitting uniforms that proclaimed their servitude. If it was a hard life for the theater workers, who at least did a job they truly loved, it was a wretched one for the palace servants. Most hated their masters. Anger and bitterness gnawed at their hearts.

Among the burdens they all bore was an overpowering need for haste. Nothing could ever be done speedily enough, and yesterday was too late for what had been ordered today. Ridj Mongo came up with a surprising solution to this problem: wheeled shoes. He and his staff took to racing up and down the halls of palace on their own wheels, bearing messages tucked into pockets or tools stored in backpacks. Soon Drax and the theater workers followed suit. More than a means to an end, the wheels became a kind of culture. Men with a competitive urge held races, while others skated for fun during their rare moments of leisure. Rowdiness became common in some quarters, especially when the masters were away in Evna. There were days when things got out of hand.

On such a day Lurline arrived in Ev.

No one at the Summer Palace realized this, or that a Magic Egg was broken just a short distance away. They knew only that suddenly, magically, and for no apparent reason, their hands and feet turned to wheels. Almost as galling, their gaudy clothes and demeaning ruffs fused with their skins—indeed became a second skin, fixed and unmovable, so that they could never change their hated garments again. It was a calamity. How could they do their jobs? Their day-to-day grudges and grumbles ignited into rage.

It was this rage that greeted Lurline when she happened onto the scene. "We gave her quite an earful." said Drax. "And who can blame us? She dropped in after the fact, when it was already too late, and she left us with nothing."

CHAPTER THIRTEEN

Matters careened inexorably from bad to worse. No hands or feet meant no jobs. Many palace servants were driven out and replaced by men from Evna. Just a few Wheelers remained, reduced to the status of living trolleys who bore burdens on their backs. Others went to Evna and found work drawing cabs and carts for pennies. A better life awaited certain theater Wheelers, especially those who could write or direct plays and those with vocal talent. Accommodations were made. But many Wheelers ended up living along the coast, scavenging lunch boxes and dinner pails and nursing their anger—endless anger, they found, when it became clear that they'd stopped aging. They lived this way for the next two hundred years. No ruler came to their aid—until Evardo.

King Evardo saw the Wheelers as fellow humans. He treated them with dignity and promoted them according to their merits. So did Queen Fluff and their daughter Runa. Runa, as patron of the Royal Theater, formed an especially close friendship with Drax and made him Artistic Director of the company. Ridj, for his part, won the respect of King Evardo and was highly regarded as head of palace staff. All prospered under their leadership. For a few golden years the immortal lives of the Wheelers grew immeasurably better.

Now Evardo was gone. Fluff had fled. Runa had landed herself in prison. Under Queen Regent Eviret, Ridj had been demoted to messenger boy while Drax was forced to masquerade as Halvan's lowly assistant.

"No one wants to live like a beast in the woods, as the angriest Wheelers do," Drax said. "But slavery is worse. That's why we're determined to act. A plan has been ripening for some time now, Jandilay, and Ridj seems to think our moment has come."

"How do you know?" asked Jandilay.

"You brought the message yourself: '*A power surge is expected and the tour must begin at once.*'"

"The tour!" Jandilay said excitedly. "Is it rebellion?"

"No," replied Drax. "Rebellion would only get us thrown into prison. Besides, we mean no harm to the people of Ev. We're talking about flight, my boy—the flight of all Wheelers and their friends from Evna. Eviret and her army wish to keep us here at all costs. She doesn't want to lose her taxi service. The one thing that can save us is the Royal Theater."

"Why can't we all just put on plays?" moaned Halvan. "No, Drax, don't tell me. I know you're right. Art without freedom is no art at all. Goodness knows I'd be glad never to do another Wheeler farce so long as I live."

"I don't understand," said Jandilay. "Drax, how can the theater help?"

"Tours! We tour constantly. Our small theaters tour Ev in covered wagons. We also share mainstage productions with the Summer Theater, and that's a much larger venture requiring many wagons. If we manage it carefully, we can smuggle Wheelers out of the city on these wagons. It's extremely dangerous. Our royal charter does not make us invulnerable. If it doesn't work on the first try, there will be no second chance. Others are in danger too, such as my friend Princess Runa, who must be freed before we go. So you see, hastiness will not do. On the other hand, there's no point waiting till we're trapped. My brother Ridj seems to think the Queen Regent has something new up her sleeve, some new power that could endanger us all. *Power surge.* I wish I knew what he meant."

"I think I do," said Jandilay. "The Magic Egg!"

CHAPTER FOURTEEN

DETOUR TO NOLAND

"I s this the city of Nole?"

"Why, what a question!" laughed the woman wheeling an empty cart. "Of course it is. Just walk through those gates up ahead and there you are. Now excuse me, I have to get home and cook dinner for my young ones."

She rejoined the steady stream of market vendors moving out from the city gates to the surrounding communities. Purple shadows flowed down out of the heights to meet them, for the sun had already dipped behind the horizon. Lights were coming on in kitchens and parlors and cooking smells filled the air. There was a homey feeling here that Evna lacked.

"We certainly are seeing the world these days," Ojo said to Button-Bright.

Button-Bright nodded. "Let's just hope this isn't a wild goose chase," he sighed.

Noland, with its capital city of Nole, had not been on their original itinerary. They'd talked the whole matter over this morning, however, and agreed that their affairs had reached a crisis. Jandilay, Grandma Natch, and Dame Zanket, to say nothing of their other friends, were all relying on them to smooth their road to Ev; but the quests they'd been given hinged on powerful and capricious people—the Red Jinn of Ev in their case—who might easily refuse to cooperate. Failure seemed entirely possible. And what then?

"We need a backup plan," Ojo had said, and Button-Bright could only concur.

That was when they remembered Noland. Both Ozma and Eviret had told them Noland was a mortal country and therefore suitable for Ozites fleeing from the burden of immortality. Would its king give them a sympathetic hearing?

"I met King Bud a long time ago," Button-Bright had said. "It was on my very first trip to Oz. He was just a boy then, only a few years older than me, and I remember liking him. He didn't put on airs or play the pampered prince. I think he's someone we can talk to."

"And isn't his sister King Evardo's wife? And hasn't she moved back in with her brother in Noland? Maybe she could help us deal with Eviret."

So it was decided: rather than going straight to Jinnicky, the boys would first make a detour to Noland and find out what alternatives might be open.

Of course, since this was a last-minute decision, Ojo had not checked the route on the Wogglebug's maps. He had a good head for maps (unlike Button-Bright) and knew the order of the countries that surrounded Oz: Ev to the northeast, Ix due north, and Noland edging out into the northwest, with Skampavia tucked in along Noland's southern border. Nole, the capital city of Noland, would be their destination. But Ojo had no clear idea of the distances involved or the landmarks they might expect to encounter. Consequently, they'd gotten a bit lost.

The confusion had started well before lunch. As the two boys in swallow form had rounded the northeast corner of the Deadly Desert, they'd seen far off what looked like a red jewel perched beside the distant Nonestic Ocean. This was in fact the Red Castle of the equally Red Jinn, but the boys had guessed it must be the City of Ix and had concluded from this that they were making excellent time. When they'd caught sight of the real City of Ix, an hour or two later, they'd decided it must be Nole. Down they'd plunged for a leisurely stroll and a Yookoohoo lunch in the city streets. It was only after they'd wasted far too much time sightseeing that they'd found out where they really were.

Off they went again, bemoaning their ill luck. It was already mid-afternoon and they still had a long way to go. When they finally reached the mountain range that separated Ix from Noland, Ojo could have kicked himself.

"I should have remembered we'd have to pass these mountains!" he said.

Button-Bright reassured him. "If it had been up to me, we'd never have gotten this far. Cheer up, Ojo! We'll be there in time for dinner."

This hopeful prediction seemed less and less likely to come true. The mountain range was high and wide, and even after they'd put it behind them they didn't know whether Nole lay to the north or the south. They tried north first, found nothing but farms and small villages, then turned around dispiritedly and flew south. Now, at last, they'd arrived. Thank goodness!

They considered flying straight to the king's palace. But this plan had caused a diplomatic crisis in Evna, so they decided that in Nole they would do it the old-fashioned way and walk through the city gates on their own boyish feet.

Traffic was mostly against them. It appeared that people from outlying neighborhoods and farms brought their goods into the city each morning and then went home again at dusk, wheeling empty carts and barrows. Only a few folks went the other way. The boys fell in with these and hoped for the best. At least the company was good. Everyone seemed to know everyone else, greeting each other by name, asking after relatives, and sharing local jokes. Though few looked wealthy, all looked so well-fed and cheerful that Ojo felt emboldened to strike up a conversation.

"Excuse me," he said to a man with a neat gray beard and dusty boots. "We're strangers here. Will we be allowed into the city?"

The man made a show of eyeing the boys up and down. "I don't know about that," he said doubtfully. "You're a desperate looking pair. Say, Master Tim!" he called to someone just ahead. A handsome young man with curly brown hair turned around. "Do you think these rascals will get past Nan at the gate?"

"Not if they're seen with the likes of you, Master Dab!" was the reply. Everyone laughed, including Master Dab.

"I'm just pulling your legs," he said to the boys. "You'll have no trouble, I promise."

And they didn't. Mistress Nan, the gatekeeper, waved them through with the others. Button-Bright thanked Master Dab and inquired what his line of work might be. Master Dab explained that he really worked in the city but sometimes took odd jobs outside when extra hands were needed. Just now the farms wanted plenty of help. "Always good to keep your hand in, eh?" he said. "If it's not sowing and reaping, it's smithing or woodworking. What about you two? What's your business in Nole?"

"We're hoping to see King Bud," Ojo told him.

Master Dab called out again. "Did you hear that, Master Tim? These gentlemen want to see the King."

Master Tim could be heard chuckling up ahead. "An excellent plan. I wish them well."

"Ah, the King," Master Dab said in a meditative tone. "Poor fellow."

"Poor fellow," several other voices repeated.

"Poor fellow? Why do you call him that? Is he unwell?"

"Unwell? No, no, he's fit as a fiddle."

"Is he in some kind of trouble?"

"Not that I know of. At least, no more than usual."

"Then why do you call him poor fellow?"

Several of Master Dab's companions turned to look. Their faces were solemn and sober. "You really don't know?" they said. "It's a terrible sorrow to us all. He's stepped off the path of life, our king has. And his sweet sister with him."

Button-Bright caught his breath. "You mean—they're dead?"

At this, Master Tim joined the conversation. "Now, now," he scolded. "You're giving these young lads the wrong impression. Anyone can see they're not from Noland and don't know our ways. Explain it to them, Dab."

Master Dab obeyed. Nolanders, he said, had always had a profound reverence for birth and death and everything that came in between—what they called the path of life. They celebrated the beginning of life, when they borrowed their physical forms from the stuff of the earth, and they celebrated the end of life, when they gave those forms back. To refuse to give them back, or to be prevented from giving them back, was for any Nolander the worst of misfortunes. This they called stepping off the path of life, by which they simply meant immortality.

Nolanders knew that Zixi, the witch queen of Ix, had become immortal long ago. The story was told that she'd once been given a Magic Egg by the fairy Lurline, and that by mixing the Egg with her own magic she'd brewed up a spell of immortality. Or, as the Nolanders said, she had stepped off the path of life. They pitied her for it.

They also knew that Zixi saw matters quite differently. To this day she placed a high value on her immortality and guarded it jealously. She had also been delighted many years ago when the fairies had granted young King Bud, the boy ruler of Noland, an extraordinary wish: to become the best king Noland ever had ("We'll see if *that* wish ever comes true!" joked Master Tim). Zixi had subsequently found in King Bud such a wise and generous neighbor that she did not wish to see him grow old and die, leaving the throne to someone less congenial. Her chance to intervene had come when she was invited to the wedding of Bud's sister, Princess Fluff, to King Evardo of Ev. Zixi's wedding present? Immortality.

But she had managed it in her own peculiar way. Rather than giving her gift to the bride and groom, as might have been expected, she had given it to the bride and her brother—Fluff and Bud. Moreover, she had cast her spell without consulting them first and had then announced it as a *fait accompli*. Both would have turned it down if they'd had any choice in the matter. Lacking that choice, they had "left the path of life," as Nolanders said.

"They're stuck here forever," Master Dab said sadly, "watching their friends grow old around them. That kind of thing may suit Zixi, but it doesn't suit a Nolander."

"Don't be so gloomy!" laughed a pretty young woman who walked alongside Master Tim. Though her masses of fair hair were tied up in a scarf, she looked so much like Tim that Button-Bright thought they must be related. "It's not that bad."

"Have it your way, Mistress Margaret," shrugged Master Dab. "Our king is a fine fellow and we're happy to keep him, as well you know. But our hearts go out to him."

"And to me too, I hope?" said Mistress Margaret. Then she clapped a hand over her mouth. "Oh! Bud, I've given us away."

General laughter greeted this. Ojo and Button-Bright stared. Bud? *King* Bud?

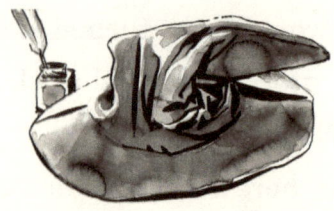

CHAPTER FIFTEEN

BUD AND FLUFF

"U nmasked!" cried Master Tim, falling against his friend Dab. "Well, these two boys would have found us out eventually. Yes, lads, I am King Bud, sometimes known as Master Tim, though I'm not master of much. And this lovely lady is my sister Fluff—sometimes known as Princess Fluff, sometimes known as Queen Fluff of Ev, sometimes known as Mistress Margaret, and always known as an incorrigible pest. Dab here is my best friend and chief councilor. At your service."

The boys were too astounded to introduce themselves properly.

"What are you doing out here?" asked Ojo. "And with spades?"

Bud, it seemed, often left the palace to run itself while he and Dab went out into the country and practiced the various trades of his people. "It's the best way keep up with things," Bud said. "You learn a lot working at a real job. Besides, palaces get awfully stuffy after a while, especially if you have to go to meetings every day. Meetings about this, meetings about that, talk talk talk. Meetings don't help me much. I think better when I'm out and about and seeing how people live. If you ever live in a palace you'll find out."

"We do live in a palace," said Button-Bright. "At least, we used to. Lately we've been out and about a lot more than we've been in. And nobody asks us to meetings."

"No meetings? Lucky fellows! Where do you come from?"

The answer to this question caused quite a sensation among the Nolanders.

"Oz?" said Dab. "That's not something we hear every day. We get visitors from all over Nonestica but almost never from Oz, what with the Deadly Desert and all. Is it true that everyone there has stepped off the path of life?"

The boys had to admit that it was. "But it's not what you're thinking," Ojo assured them. "When everybody's immortal together there's no problem."

The Nolanders shook their heads and tsked sadly. "Poor lads," they said. "What a brave face they put on it, and all the time you can see their young hearts are breaking. It's a cruel fate, a cruel fate."

140

The boys exchanged glances of utter befuddlement. This was a view of immortality they'd never heard before. They did not consider themselves to be in need of anyone's pity and their young hearts weren't breaking. But as they walked through the twilit streets that led to the palace, it occurred to them that there was a very promising aspect to the whole thing. If these kind-hearted Nolanders and their hard-working king placed such a high value on mortality, they might be persuaded to welcome an occasional like-minded Ozite—even, perhaps, the cantankerous Dame Zanket. With this in mind, they launched into an account of their mission.

They did not get far, however. The first mention of Ev brought the Nolanders up short.

"Ev?" Fluff said excitedly. "You say you've been in Ev? What's the news there? Have you brought us a message from Jinnicky?"

They hadn't brought a message, she was disappointed to learn. And the news they brought did not encourage her. Indeed, when they told her they were trying to help the Queen Regent, she at once grew cold and distant. "Even Oz serves my daughter's purposes!" she said bitterly. "What hope is there for my poor husband?"

This took the boys by surprise. While they couldn't have said positively that they *liked* Queen Regent Eviret, or that they relished her companionship, they certainly hadn't expected her own mother to adopt this attitude.

Bud cautioned his sister. "Remember, Fluff, most folks don't know Eviret the way you do. You've said yourself she can talk her way around anybody. She had us all fooled for years. Besides, maybe these boys have turned up just in time to help us all out. Let's talk it over tonight and hear what they have to say."

"Talk it over?" echoed Dab. "Why, Master Tim! Am I hearing things or did you just schedule a meeting?"

Everyone burst into laughter, none more cheerfully than the king himself.

In spite of all this, however, it turned out that there could be no meeting that night.

"Bud!" Fluff shouted over the noise. "Aren't you forgetting something? We've got the MMBBG tonight. We won't even be in bed till about one!"

Laughter turned to howls of outsized woe. Bud slapped his forehead despairingly. Why, he wanted to know, had no one reminded him that MMBBG night should never be preceded by a day of hard labor? "Will they at least wait while we get cleaned up?" he asked.

"If they're wise they'll insist on it," Dab said drily. "Here's the palace door. Everybody inside, please, before the door wards change their minds and lock us all out for vagrants. You too, Oz lads."

The boys had been so absorbed in their new companions that they'd forgotten to notice their surroundings. Now they found themselves hurrying out of the deepening gloom of the street into a cheerful, well-lit foyer with a blazing fire. Tomorrow, if they were still here, they'd have to take time to examine the place.

"What's the MBG?" asked Ojo, following the others up a flight of stairs.

"MMBBG," Bud corrected him. "The Milk Maids and Buttery Boys Guild, if you must know. Very important people. I know how hard they work because I've done those jobs. We throw them an annual dinner just to say thank you, and I'm afraid it happens to be tonight—the one time there's a meeting I actually want to go to! Can we put off our talk till tomorrow morning? We'll find rooms for you, and in the morning you can join Fluff and me for breakfast. Say, would you two care to help out? We're just serving and washing up—and believe me, that's enough. My sister is a stern taskmaster."

The boys looked at one another and grinned. They were going to spend the night anyway, and they had nothing else to occupy them. How hard could it be? "Tell us what to do and we'll do it," said Button-Bright.

Fluff eyed them. "You have no idea what you're letting yourself in for," she said. "Get yourselves clean, everybody, and suit up. The MMBBG is going to run us all off our feet!"

CHAPTER SIXTEEN

FLUFF MAKES IT ALL TOO CLEAR

Fluff was not joking. Out of the palace kitchens came six kinds of salad, as many soups, more appetizers than anyone could count, a dozen main courses, and a dazzling array of pies, cakes and ices. The milk maids and buttery boys weren't shy and made it their business to try a little (or a lot) of everything. The wait staff had all it could do to keep up with them.

In addition to Bud, Dab, and the boys, the wait staff included all five of the remaining council members, together with their various assistants and hangers-on. Princess Fluff took command of the forces, as well as doing her own share of the work, and by dessert time they had all become fast friends.

"Nothing quite like this happens in Oz," Button-Bright said to Dab during a brief lull.

"King Bud has never been the ivory tower type," replied Dab. "He's apprenticed himself to every kind of trade you can think of—including buttery boy. Outside the city no one calls him 'Your Majesty.' No, it's 'Master Tim' when he's out of his royal robes. And all that's in addition to running his kingdom! He's a wonder, our king. Poor fellow."

King Bud overhead this. He'd just been mopping up an overturned punch bowl and was now teetering under an armful of wet towels. "Don't let Dab fool you," he laughed." The truth is I get bored easily and can't help making a pest of myself."

The guests ended their evening with many lustily sung songs, several of which affectionately lampooned the King. "No ifs, ands or Buds," went one chorus. "Sweet as a rosebud," went another. His love of pranks was celebrated in a song called "The Bud of All Jokes." Even the ex-Queen of Ev came in for a bit of ribbing in a song called "Well, Did You Ev-ah."

At the end of it all, when the leftovers had been packed up and the seemingly endless dishes washed, the Ozites slept soundly in a little second-story room they'd been given. And when they awoke next morning, it was to broad daylight and a fresh breeze streaming in through their open window. With these came an irresistible smell of pancakes and maple syrup. The boys wasted no time but washed, dressed, and hurried downstairs.

Breakfast had been set on a cozy little terrace overlooking the garden. Bud, Fluff, and Dab were just pouring hot chocolate when their guests burst onto the scene.

"All meetings should be like this," the King said feelingly when they'd exchanged their good mornings and taken their seats. "Then I wouldn't dread them quite so much. Now, first things first. Fluff, you have something to say?"

Fluff stood up. She'd let her hair down and it floated in a light brown cloud over her shoulders. Her face, however, wore a solemn expression.

"Thanks, Bud," she said. "The fact is, I owe our two guests an apology."

They looked at her in surprise. Why should she apologize to them?

"It's because of that long face I pulled when you told us you're helping Eviret. It was unfair of me. Eviret is my daughter, you see, and her little tricks stopped working on me a long time ago. But I know how persuasive she can be, especially to strangers. It's obvious you two have fallen under her spell. You're hardly the first and you won't be the last. But last night it just broke my heart. I'm sorry if I was rude."

The boys assured her there was no need for apologies. At the same time, they didn't understand what Fluff meant by a spell. "Eviret told us she had no magic," Button-Bright said. "Was she lying? Did she work some kind of charm on us?"

"Not the kind of charm you mean," said Fluff. "But a charm nevertheless. We all cast little spells every time we speak, every time we tell a story in this way rather than that way. It's the magic of persuasion. My daughter Eviret is very good at it. Let me tell you my own story in my own way and then you can judge for yourselves."

Though Fluff had been young and untraveled when she first left Noland and moved to Ev as King Evardo's queen, she had quickly grown to love her adopted country and its honest, hardworking Evites. She loved her husband, who had ruled Ev wisely and well. Together they'd made it their goal to heal Ev of Mad Evoldo's many hurts and transform it into a loving and compassionate country. They'd established friendly relations with their neighbor to the north, the Red Jinn, as well as seeing to it that prosperity benefitted everyone and that humans and Wheelers lived together in peace.

Success in Evna, however, had not meant success at home. The royal couple's eldest daughter, Eviret, had unfortunately taken after her infamous grandfather, Evoldo the Mad. Their efforts to tame her selfishness and conceit had been in vain.

She'd also had a way with words. Even as a very little girl, she'd known how to turn her own bad behavior into an epic about how neglected and humiliated she was and how mean and spiteful everyone else was. She had made herself believed, too. Wheeler servants had borne the brunt of her youthful machinations. Later she had worked her wiles on poor Runa.

Time went by. Evardo and Fluff had gradually come to understand Eviret and had learned not to take her lies and distortions at face value. This had annoyed and frustrated the young princess, who blamed Runa and the Wheelers when she didn't get her way and brooded ceaselessly over her imagined wrongs. She had also laid secret plans, and when the time was right she had put them into action.

Where she got the sleeping spell no one knew for certain. It had never actually been proven that she was behind it at all. Some said one thing, some another. Either way, at the hale, hardy, still vigorous age of seventy-five, King Evardo had suddenly fallen into an endless sleep.

Then things had changed in a hurry. The line of succession was clear: neither the king's heartbroken wife nor any of his bereaved brothers and sisters could take charge. Only his eldest offspring could do that—and Eviret did, with a vengeance. It helped that she'd been secretly cultivating a cozy relationship with the Royal Guard, aided and abetted by her Uncle Evington, and that she now used the royal coffers to buy the Guard's loyalty. No one could oppose her when she rolled back her parents' reforms. The old dungeons were opened and put back into use. Servants loyal to Evardo were sent away. Fear and mistrust returned to Evna—most of all to the Queen Regent herself.

Then came the event that confirmed her worst fears: Evanna and Fluff absconded with the sleeping King Evardo.

It was to achieve this that Queen Fluff had stayed so long. The spell that gripped her husband, she knew, would never be broken while Eviret was in charge. So Fluff, Runa, and Evanna conspired with the Royal Theater to smuggle the king out of the palace, out of Evna, and away to the Red Jinn's castle.

"Now I sit here, useless," Fluff sighed. "It can't go on this way."

Silence fell. The echoes of this sad story seemed to linger in the fresh morning air. Ojo and Button-Bright sat stunned.

"I can't believe we let her fool us," Ojo said.

"It was all right in front of us," said Button-Bright. "Why didn't we see it?"

Dab shook his head sadly. "Don't take it to heart, boys. You heard what Fluff said. Eviret is very good at fooling people. We've all had to learn this the hard way."

"You don't understand," Button-Bright said miserably. "It's worse than you think. Princess Runa has been sent to the dungeons!"

Fluff caught her breath. "The old dungeons? My Runa? Oh, I was afraid this would happen! Why did I let her stay behind when I knew how dangerous it was? Bud, we've got to get her out!"

Bud agreed. "We'll do it, Fluff. Eviret is a royal pain but she's not invincible."

"She *wasn't* invincible," said Ojo.

The time had come to reveal the worst news of all—how Eviret had found out about Magic Eggs. "She'd never even heard of a Magic Egg was till we came along," Ojo said sorrowfully. "Now she wants one for herself."

"And Onna Val has flown off to get it!" Button-Bright added. "For all we know she might have it already. She might be on her way to the Red Castle right now!"

No one wanted to see power of that kind at Eviret's disposal. "Let's hope Lurline keeps her Magic Eggs locked up tight," said Dab.

"We can't count on that," said Fluff. "We can't count on anything. Oh, Bud! Do you know what I want most of all? I want to wake up my husband! I miss him so much. If only we had him back, there would be no more of this Queen Regent nonsense. Even the Royal Guard knows that Evardo is the rightful King of Ev."

"King Evardo is in danger too," said Button-Bright. "Eviret told us to bring him back to her. But if she gets a Magic Egg, she won't wait for that. She'll go to the Red Castle and get him herself. She said so."

Bud squared his shoulders. "That's enough for me. Fluff, you're right. Evardo is the real key to the whole thing.

We've got to get him disenchanted. What do you say we all pay a visit on our friend Jinnicky?"

Fluff gave her brother a hug. She was ready to leave that very second.

"It's a long trip," Dab pointed out. "It'll take days."

"We can fix that!" Ojo and Button-Bright cried out in unison.

CHAPTER SEVENTEEN
THE RULERS OF AN

"I'm afraid not," said Lurline.

"Under no circumstances!" barked her brother Jinjin.

"But you *have* to!" Onna Val pleaded. She was growing hoarse. How long had she been haranguing them now? One hour? Two hours? She had found the rulers of An in a secluded palace garden where they often discussed their plans, and there she had told them the whole story twice through, with enough Italics to shame even the Queen Regent. She had told the history of Ev too, as far as she knew it, laying the heaviest possible stress upon the unfair distribution of immortality, the unworthiness of the Wheelers, and the blame Lurline deserved for all of it.

Couldn't they see? A Magic Egg was the only answer! They *had* to give her one—or take it to Ev themselves.

And if that weren't enough, she also invoked Jandilay's past service. Only he, in his last act as a Phanfasm, had had strength enough to force Jinjin into the Truth Pond with his sister so that both could be made whole again. This one deed was now honored throughout the realm, for it alone had made possible the restoration of An. Wasn't that worth a Magic Egg?

None of it seemed to matter. Lurline looked regretful and apologetic. Jinjin looked stern. Neither showed any sign of relenting.

"I will pass no judgment on Cloudcourt and its work with the Magic Eggs," Jinjin said (rather unconvincingly, Onna Val thought). "It belongs to the sad years of our estrangement, when all that we did turned to bitterness. Now those years have ended."

"Thanks to Jandilay!"

"Yes," said Lurline. "Thanks to Jandilay. But be that as it may, the days of the Magic Eggs will not return. Be content, Onna Val. We cannot give you what you ask, not even for the friend you love."

"Is that what I'm supposed to tell Eviret?" Onna Val demanded. "That you know you botched Ev the first time, but now you're out of the Egg business, so never mind?"

CHAPTER SEVENTEEN

A look of sorrow crossed Lurline's fair young face. Before her momentous dip in the Truth Pond, this ageless fairy had been a beautiful and stately woman, seemingly about thirty-five years old. So she had appeared long ages ago when she'd set out on the Cloudcourt Experiment and commenced breaking Magic Eggs and creating fairylands all over the world. Her brother Jinjin had likewise appeared as a man in his full prime, handsome, strong, and sternly opposed to any and all Egg-breaking. The Truth Pond had made both of them younger and fresher, their natures less sharply opposed.

"I regret what happened in Ev," Lurline admitted. "Yet there were reasons for it. Your friend Eviret says I should have broken the Magic Egg further south, where most of her people lived. Perhaps. But below Ev's southern border lived the Phanfasms and Mimics, evil spirits of great power. To break an Egg near their country might have increased their power tenfold."

Onna Val hesitated. She knew about the Phanfasms and realized what a potent argument this was. But Eviret's wrongs had etched themselves into her heart and could not yet be erased by mere facts.

"It's not *fair!*" she insisted. "*Everyone* got immortality except the Ev people. The Wheelers got it. The Red Jinn got it."

At this Lurline shook her head. "Ah, the Red Jinn. There I can promise you your Queen Regent is absolutely wrong. No Magic Egg had any effect on Jinnicky. What he was then, what he still is now, is neither more nor less than what he made himself: utterly impervious, the pure product and expression of his own Red Magic."

"True," said her brother. "The Red Jinn is a law unto himself. It's even possible that Ev's Magic Egg fizzled because of him."

"Only the Wheelers were changed by it," Lurline continued. "And they are a problem that's easily solved."

"They are? How?"

"Your friend Button-Bright could restore them to their original forms, if they wish it. It's just the sort of magic he's good at."

Onna Val was taken aback. She knew perfectly well that Button-Bright was an expert at transformation. Why hadn't they thought of this themselves? While she stood silent, Jinjin rose.

"Sister, we're expected at the greenhouse. There is work to be done."

"There always is. Onna Val, offer our simple remedy to Ev's Queen Regent. If she accepts it, you and Jandilay will remain there as long as you choose. If not—well, there's nothing else we can do. But whatever happens, remember that you and Jandilay always have a home with us."

They swept out side by side, the reconciled sister and brother.

Onna Val stood thinking over what she'd heard. A simple transformation: was that really all it would take to restore the Wheelers? And if so, what should she feel? Relieved, because an easy, safe solution had been found? Triumphant, because her friend Button-Bright could make it happen? She felt neither of those things. Worse still, she feared that Eviret wouldn't either. But why wouldn't she? Where was the catch that would spoil it all and cause the Queen Regent to turn poor Jandilay out of her kingdom?

Onna Val jumped up. Of course! Immortality! Wheeled or not, the Wheelers had been made forever and always immortal, while rank and file Evites—to say nothing of the royal family—had not. It was grossly unfair and no pretty words from Lurline and Jinjin could change that. Eviret had been right all along. She *must* have a Magic Egg! Onna Val *owed* it to her.

Where to get one? Lurline's whole stock of Magic Eggs had never been used up, of that Onna Val was sure. But where had she put them? Someplace well hidden, no doubt. Could Onna Val find them? Possibly. She possessed an uncanny knack for finding hidden things. But she had no time to waste and the consequences of defying her rulers in this crucial matter would be dire. No, Lurline's hiding place must be left untouched. Was there another source? Where had Lurline gotten her Magic Eggs to begin with?

"The Phoenix," Onna Val whispered.

She caught her breath. Had she really just said that?

It was a stupendous thing to contemplate. Only Lurline herself had made the journey up into the mountains where the Phoenix lived. No other fairy, so far as they knew, had ever seen the Phoenix. And what *was* the Phoenix? Only the oldest of all birds in this ancient fairyland, the fabled wonder whose eggs contained the pure, raw essence of fairy magic. Could Onna Val go alone to the Phoenix? Did she dare?

Even as these thoughts flashed through her mind, she was already racing in search of warmer clothes. She had not a moment to lose.

CHAPTER EIGHTEEN

MOUNT PHOENIX

Though legends concerning the Phoenix itself were annoyingly vague, legends concerning its location were crystal clear. In the north of An rose a jumble of rugged peaks called the Phoenix Mountains, and out of that jumble rose the highest peak of all: Mt. Phoenix itself, perpetually snowcapped and utterly desolate. That was where the Phoenix lived. That was where Onna Val had to go. She leaned into her traveling cloud and urged it on.

She had already urged it to impossible feats that very morning. The journey from Ev to An ordinarily took her twelve hours at normal speeds; today she had done it in five. The hair had been all but torn from her head. If only Lurline had done the right thing and given her what she wanted!

Then Onna Val could have hustled the Magic Egg back to Ev by late evening and the whole problem would have been solved. But no, all her efforts had left the fairy queen unconvinced. Half a day wasted! And now she had to take this extra trip to Mt. Phoenix. Even if her quest proved successful, she couldn't possibly make it back to Ev tonight. She would just have to wait till tomorrow. Her heart raced with frustration.

This journey would be daunting. Two thick sweaters and an even thicker coat sat beside her. Boots, gloves, leggings, scarves, and a wool cap completed her gear. Beyond these, only her native wits could help her.

The landscape

streaked away beneath her. Eastward she saw the twin valleys of Estram and Tamser, separated by low hills. Ahead lay the lush, green-fringed course of the river. Beyond that, among the fertile foothills, the Dragon and his many descendants made their homes. Onna Val considered asking their advice, then thought better of it. She had no time for their endless, rambling digressions and reminiscences, which in any case would probably end in crushing disapproval. She must do this on her own.

Nearer and nearer drew the mountains. Now their broken feet lay beneath her. The lower slopes filled her gaze. She charted a zigzag path among them, rising steadily higher and higher as she went. When it grew cold, she stopped just long enough to put on the leggings and the sweaters. Then on she went, up and up, deeper and deeper into the remotest regions where icy winds whistled about her. Thank goodness there were no storms or fogs today! She stopped again and put on the coat, the hat, the scarves, and the gloves. Her nose felt like an icicle.

She glanced back. The whole world lay spread out far below her. No, not the whole world. Just An—Lurline's fairyland, now reduced to a formless, featureless haze, dreaming of its own importance.

What really mattered lay ahead and above—Mt. Phoenix, rearing a lonely pyramid of rock and snow high above its nearest rivals. She followed a circular path around it, scanning its white slopes and black cliffs for some sign of avian life. Just what to look for she did not know, but seeking and finding were in her blood. She tore the glove from her right hand and stretched out her bare fingers. Higher, they told her. Still higher.

Now sharp left. She peered ahead and saw nothing but black and white, white and black. Or was that...? Yes! A splash of shimmering green floated amid the desolation. She made for it. It grew as she approached, resolving itself into— what? A grassy knoll? No, those were leaves—the tiny, massed leaves of a great willow tree, its thick tendrils hanging in curtains down to the ground. The trunk of the tree could barely be seen. What was a willow tree doing in this lifeless place? Yet here it stood, serene and still, unruffled by the buffeting winds. It had to be what she sought.

She landed, climbed down from her cloud, and parted the leafy curtain.

Within the air was warm and dry. The howling voice of the mountain could have been miles and miles away. Strange, sweet smells filled her nostrils and a gentle radiance drifted down from somewhere overhead. She took off the hat, the scarves, and the remaining glove. She took off her coat, too, and one of the sweaters. She peered up into the tree.

"I hear something," said a voice overhead. "Is it the girl you were going on about a moment ago?"

"I have no idea what you mean," a second voice replied. "What girl?"

"What girl indeed. You couldn't stop talking about her. Now I suppose you've forgotten the matter. Your memory is as bad as ever."

"True. That's why I keep *you* around. No doubt you'll remember this girl after she leaves. Then you can tell me all about her."

"If there's anything to tell. It'll be a very short account unless she decides to speak."

Onna Val could see nothing. Where were the voices coming from? And were they the voices of men or women? Or both at once? She said loudly, "I wish you wouldn't talk about me as if I'm not here!"

"If you are here, you can hardly expect us to know it."

"*I* know for a fact there was no one here a few minutes ago."

"And *I'm* certain there will be no one here a few minutes from now."

Something shifted among the leaves overhead. Onna Val peered. There! Something sat among the leaves, blending with them so perfectly that it could only be seen when it moved. Something rounded and smooth—a green-plumaged body. Out of the body—was it possible?—grew not one but two graceful necks. And out of each neck grew an even more graceful head. The two heads appeared exactly identical, with their long, straight beaks and their green crests. Neither spared a glance for Onna Val.

"How can you not know I'm here?" she asked. "I'm standing right under your tree. Are you blind?"

"Not in the least!"

"What a crude thing to say. Blind indeed."

"I see perfectly well when I'm considering the rich and varied wonders of the past."

"And when *I'm* contemplating the mysteries and complexities of the future, my vision gives me no trouble at all."

"No trouble? Don't make me laugh. You have a great deal of trouble, as you're always complaining. There are so many futures that you can't possibly keep them all sorted out. When the egg fairy asked you about them you couldn't give her a straight answer."

"Couldn't I? Well, who could, after all? It's a perfect tangle. But I see it all the same. There's no need to speak of blindness. It's only the present that we can't see."

"Exactly so. And the present, after all, is such a paltry thing. Over in a flash. Poof! Let us not speak of it."

"Naturally not. Whatever would we say?"

"There's nothing *to* say."

"Nothing whatever."

Silence fell. Onna Val wondered if she'd been dismissed.

"That girl," one of the heads said after a moment. "She did arrive. I remember now. She came indoors and took off her things. It's possible that she's still here."

"Of course I'm still here!" cried Onna Val. "Why can't you see me?"

"I distinctly remember answering that question a moment ago. Really, girl, your memory seems as bad as my other self's. *I* look only into the past. *He* looks only into the future. It's perfectly simple. Please don't make me say it again."

"She's not going to make you say it again," the other head said suddenly. "She's going to ask us for one of our eggs. *That's* something new, isn't it? I can't remember that happening before."

"You can't remember *anything*! I'm amazed that you're not constantly after me to introduce myself. Of course someone's asked for our eggs before! The egg fairy did, hundreds of years ago now. It was all she wanted to talk about. Surprisingly limited in her interests. We gave her one egg on her first visit, as I recall, and two on her second. On her third visit she brought a basket and filled the whole thing. Cleared the place out a bit. I was happy to get rid of so many. Too bad more have come along since then."

"Have they? I wouldn't know."

Onna Val frowned. The Phoenix seemed not to realize how powerful and perilous its eggs were. It regarded them as mere clutter! This was good news for Onna Val's immediate purpose, of course, but still...

"Shouldn't you be taking better care of your eggs?" she admonished the creature.

The two heads looked at each other and rolled their eyes.

"I don't see why," said one. "What's done is done."

"And what will be done is—well, let's just say it's another matter entirely. You'll get your egg, if that's what you want to know. Anything beyond that is, if you'll pardon the expression, none of your business."

"But anyone can walk in here!" Onna Val persisted. "It's too easy!"

"Easy for you. Not so easy for someone else."

"Why easy for me? Do you mean you were you expecting me?"

"Why, I've never expected anything as long as I've lived!"

"And if I *had* expected it, you could hardly imagine I'd remember doing so. Really, girl, you are awfully dense."

"Oh, for goodness sake!" said Onna Val. She had had enough of this strangely circuitous conversation. What was the good of a creature that could see into the past and the future but could bring neither to bear on the present? Washing her hands of the whole affair, she decided to find her Magic Egg and get out. She didn't need to look far. Near the base of the willow tree was a large hollow, and in the hollow she found about half a dozen Magic Eggs. They looked just the way she remembered them: not much larger than her clenched fist and as gray as ash. As vessels of raw fairy magic they had always cut a poor figure.

She only wanted one. She made her choice, put it into her coat pocket, and began piling on her winter gear again.

"It's lovely to be alone again," sighed one of the Phoenix's two heads.

"Idiot," said the other.

Before she left, Onna Val almost asked whether things would turn out all right for her and Jandilay. But what good would that do? If the future were as tangled as the Phoenix had said, there wouldn't be much point. Besides, her immediate future was clear. She would spend the night at Lurline's palace (no one had to know where she'd been), then return to Ev in the morning.

"I make my own future," she said to herself. And she plunged back out into the cold.

CHAPTER NINETEEN

GOING ON TOUR

fire?" echoed the Queen Regent.

"That's right," said Halvan. He had joined Eviret and Jandilay for breakfast and was playing with his food in a preoccupied manner. He dug a little well in the center of his oatmeal and then watched while it slowly filled up with blueberry syrup. "Our friends at the Summer Theater are just about to open their season. They've chosen a favorite of yours, *Wheelers on Parade*. But it seems they've accidentally burned up the whole production— backdrops, props, puppets, everything. So they'd like to borrow ours. Naturally I'm eager to help out." He dug a little trench along the side of his oatmeal. The syrup oozed back out again. "We'll have to spend the entire day loading eight wagons. Jandilay won't mind helping me shop for supplies. And you'll loan us your six carriage Wheelers, won't you? With luck I'll send the wagons out first thing in the morning. You might warn the gatekeepers."

Jandilay held his breath. Would the Queen Regent accept this?

She sighed extravagantly. "Oh, if people only *knew* the unglamorous lives we all live behind the scenes!" she said. "I don't know how I *bear* it! Yes, yes, take your wagons out of the city. Evington will see to the gates. Now *please* let's talk about something interesting or I'll never digest my *breakfast!*"

"That's one hurdle," Halvan whispered to Jandilay when they'd finished and rushed off. "Only a few dozen to go. Onward!"

It would be an exhausting day. The escape of Evna's Wheelers had begun! Jandilay himself had precipitated the commotion when he revealed the true nature and power of a Magic Egg. Halvan and Drax Mongo had been so alarmed that they'd decided not to wait any longer. Much had to be done and all had to look like the normal hustle and bustle of a theater company setting out on tour.

Supplies were just the beginning. Secret instructions must percolate out among the local Wheeler population, so that they would understand what to do and when to do it. The six borrowed Wheelers had ways of managing this even in the midst of a breathless shopping spree, and the pace they set kept the whole group busy all morning. The work got more and more arduous because Halvan and Jandilay constantly loaded up carts and barrows with goods such as food, water, rope, and other items. Pulling the carts was the Wheelers' job. No one who observed all this could have doubted that the Wheelers were working hard for their human masters. Necessity became camouflage.

When they delivered everything to the Scene Shop, they found the place already humming. Locals saw nothing unusual in the frenzy of activity for all tours typically commenced here. Behind the scenes, though, Jandilay finally learned what the venture entailed and how much advance planning had gone into it.

Every wagon in the theater's fleet had a false bottom. These false bottoms were dark, cramped, narrow spaces accessed by hidden doors, completely invisible when shut. When the time came to set out, all Wheelers not engaged in pulling the wagons would crawl into these spaces and remain there while they made their way out of the city. It would be a dangerous, uncomfortable journey. If the plot were discovered they would be helpless to defend themselves. Meanwhile, basic supplies and theatrical equipment went on top of the wagons, for the ruse would convince no one unless a very real production of *Wheelers on Parade* could be seen in all its disassembled glory.

Jandilay helped throughout the afternoon, following the instructions of humans and Wheelers alike. It was during this time that he realized how universally and wholeheartedly the theater community embraced the mad scheme. Yesterday he had formed a vague impression that Halvan and Drax Mongo were going it alone, or perhaps with minimal help. This was not so. Every single person in every single department understood what was at stake, both for the escaping Wheelers and for themselves.

He soon found himself reunited with Vigo and Virra, the puppeteers he had met when he and his friends first arrived. They shook his hand delightedly.

"All this is completely insane, you know," Vigo told him.

"Isn't it just!" agreed Virra. "But that's theater for you. Does it make any kind of sense? No. Is there any wisdom in it? Not a scrap. Yet without it nobody's life is worth living. We do it because we must, and that's that. Hand me that crate there, will you?"

Jandilay felt proud that he'd been taken into their confidence. He only wished he could do more to help.

"We'll make use of you, never fear," said Drax Mongo. "For one thing, you'll have to keep the Queen Regent off guard at dinner tonight. No one will envy you that!"

Jandilay's heart sank. Amid the hustle and bustle he'd forgotten that he was still expected to dine at the palace. Could he bear the sound of Eviret's voice chattering on and on about nothing? Over the past two days he'd grown to detest the woman so much that he would far rather have locked her in her bedroom and thrown away the key.

"But I'm going with you, aren't I?" he implored Drax. "When you escape?"

Drax nodded. "No one can be left behind. Where a few go, all must go. Meanwhile, you'll have a far more dangerous job. I can't tell you what it is yet. It's a job only you and my brother can do." Jandilay pressed him in vain. "Have dinner with the Queen Regent, give her no cause for suspicion, and then go back to your room. Sleep if you can. Ridj Mongo will come for you later."

Twilight had fallen by the time Jandilay left the Shop. As he walked, he wondered what his dangerous job would be. He couldn't imagine. The guards let him into the palace and he made his way up to the Queen Regent's dining chamber. Bracing himself, he opened the door.

"Look who's here!" sang Eviret's voice. The next moment, to his horror, he was being hugged by a jubilant Onna Val.

"Jandilay, Jandilay!" she cried, her face alight with joy. Eviret and Captain Evington sat at the table behind her. "I did it! Lurline and Jinjin wouldn't help, so I went to the Phoenix myself. Can you believe it? The Phoenix! It was so strange, I'll tell you about it later. Anyway, I did it! We're home free!"

She dragged him to the table and sat him down. He barely saw the food laid out in front of him. He'd been so busy he'd all but forgotten Onna Val and her mission. Or if he had thought about it, he wouldn't have expected her back so soon.

"You—you got it? The Magic Egg?"

She laughed. "Don't be so surprised. I *had* to do it. Nothing could have stopped me. We live in Ev now, Jandilay. And we work for the Royal Theater. It's all set! Try the noodles, they're delicious."

This was awful. With Eviret listening to every word, how could he explain?

"What about Ojo and Button-Bright? Weren't they supposed to...?" He couldn't remember any longer what their quest had been.

Eviret dismissed them with a snap of her fingers. "We don't need *them*!" she exulted. "I have my *own* Magic Egg now! Tonight the kitchen staff will help me bake it into a *loaf*. Or perhaps a crescent roll. I do *love* crescent rolls, with lots of butter and jam." There was a plateful on the table. She helped herself to one and devoured it with relish.

"A magic crescent roll won't be easy to divide in half," Evington said meaningly. "Wouldn't a loaf be better?"

Eviret's face went blank for a moment. "Half? Oh, so you can have *your* share. Well, yes. Yes, Uncle Evington, you're quite right. How silly of me. That's *exactly* what I'll do. You'll get yours. For *breakfast* tomorrow." She popped the last bite of her roll into her mouth. "Won't that be something! 'What did you have for breakfast this morning?' 'Oh, I had a nice slice of *immortality*. It was *divine!*'" The Queen Regent uttered her braying laugh. Jandilay shuddered. "But immortality is just the beginning. I'll be the most powerful person in *Ev!* I'll be more powerful than the Red Jinn *himself!* I'll go to the Red Castle first thing tomorrow morning and take back my father—by *force*, if necessary. Oh, and there's one other thing I'd *so* like. I'd like to know the mind of *every* single person who thinks unkind thoughts about me. That would fox *them*, wouldn't it? They could never hide their *awful* little plots again. *So* handy!"

"I'm going to help," said Onna Val. "In the kitchen, I mean, with the Magic Egg. Jandilay, you won't mind being alone tonight, will you? And tomorrow we'll move to the theater. Isn't it wonderful?"

Jandilay's heart was breaking. Onna Val had done all this for him out of pure friendship—and it was an unmitigated catastrophe! How could he let her help the Queen Regent? Worse still, how could he think of leaving Evna without her? He couldn't. Yet how could they stay? And now a terrible thought struck him. The theater would close! It would have to. All the workers were going into exile. Anyone rash enough to linger would be thrown into prison. He and Onna Val had found paradise at the exact moment when it destroyed itself for the greater good. And Onna Val had no idea! She clearly believed that she was doing the right thing.

Fortunately he didn't have to say much during dinner. Eviret liked to dominate every conversation and certainly dominated this one. She probably couldn't have stopped talking if she'd wanted to. She was madly impatient.

"I can't *wait* to get my hands on that Egg!" she gloated. "*No* one else must break it. That privilege will be *mine* alone. Hurry, everyone, I'm absolutely on pins and *needles!*"

They finished dinner in record time. Jandilay tried to corner Onna Val, but to no avail. He wasn't even sure what he would say to her. *"Whatever you do, for goodness sake try to ruin that Magic Egg?"* She would probably think he'd gone crazy.

It made no difference. Eviret hustled the girl away toward the kitchens, talking a mile a minute. After they'd gone, Jandilay went back to his room, fell onto the bed fully dressed, and cried himself to sleep.

CHAPTER TWENTY

THE PRISONER

D id the knocking wake him up, or had he been lying awake feeling miserable? Jandilay never knew. He stumbled to the door and opened it.

"Be as quiet as you can," whispered Ridj Mongo. He was wearing his saddlebags. They bulged. "The whole palace should be asleep right now, but lights are blazing down in the kitchens. We'll have to be extra careful." He refused to say what their task was. Instead he took Jandilay on a devious route that led up, down, and around, till Onna Val herself couldn't have said what was north, south, east, or west. At last they took a side stairway down to a sub-basement, then yet another stairway that dove beneath that.

Ridj's wheels were in such constant danger of slipping that Jandilay often had to brace him.

At the bottom they found a locked door with an unconscious guard sprawled in front of it.

"No, he's not dead," Ridj whispered in response to Jandilay's questioning look. "Just very, very drunk. An old trick, but an effective one. Now look in my saddlebags for a set of keys." Jandilay did so, and found the one that opened the locked door. They stepped over the sleeping guard.

After one final stairway, eerily torchlit, they entered a narrow hallway built entirely of stone. The air was foul. Two more guards lay in soggy heaps along the wall.

"What is this place?" Jandilay whispered. But he already guessed the answer.

"The old dungeon," Ridj whispered back. "We're rescuing my best friend."

"Just like old times."

"What?"

Jandilay gave a slight shiver. "In my days as a Phanfasm, I helped many poor souls out of worse places than this. I had magical powers then. Now I have none."

"Then we must do without," said Ridj. If any of this surprised him, he did not show it.

Another key opened another door. Even torchlight could not penetrate the darkness beyond. Jandilay hesitated. He heard something or someone moving out of sight.

"Who's there?" demanded a woman's voice. "Am I to die now?"

"No, dear Princess Runa. It's me, Ridj Mongo. We're getting you out of here."

There was a cry of joy as the two greeted each other.

"Oh, Ridj! I thought I'd never see you again. But what are you doing down here? You'll be taken!"

"Not tonight. The guards are all asleep. We're going on tour!"

"What—*the* tour? Tonight?"

"Yes, my dear. All our dreams are finally coming true. And we're taking you with us. Can you walk? A friend is with me. Let him help you."

Princess Runa felt weak and stiff from her confinement. Under Ridj Mongo's direction, and in almost total darkness, Jandilay helped her into fresh clothes from the saddlebags. There was food and water for the unfortunate woman. As she ate, Ridj told Jandilay more about her.

"This is Princess Runa, the King's younger daughter. Would that she had been the elder and heir to the throne! She has been a great friend to me and to all my kind. It's due to her that we have a plan at all."

"Don't exaggerate, Ridj," the Princess said wryly.

"I wouldn't think of it. You stayed behind, in terrible danger, when your mother fled. You gave us everything we needed for this day. We Wheelers will never forget it."

"My mother played her own part. So did many others—including, it seems, your helper here. Friend, please tell me your name so I can thank you properly for your kindness."

Jandilay introduced himself as best he could, but there was little time for thanks.

"We must go," said Ridj. "Your hood, Princess. Now lean on Jandilay."

A surreal journey ensued. Jandilay could not rid himself of the feeling that he'd wakened from a sunlit dream, only to find himself back on the Mountain Phantastico. Darkness and menace were the only reality. He remembered how his maimed and broken heart had almost burst with brief happiness on those rare occasions when he'd managed to save someone's life. Now his heart was whole again. The weight of Runa's arm across his shoulders, and the trust that she placed in him, made him feel he would walk through fire for this stranger he had never so much as heard of before tonight, whose face he still had not seen. At all costs the courageous Princess must be made safe.

Afterward, Jandilay decided, he would come back for his friend Onna Val. He had to.

A secret tunnel brought them to a hidden alley just outside the palace. "We're not far from the Shop," Ridj whispered. "It's just a few blocks now." Between the two of them they managed to keep the Princess upright, stumbling as best they could from shadow to shadow, shunning the lamplight. No one else walked abroad at this hour, yet the very emptiness seemed watchful. Their footsteps echoed uncannily in the night.

Tour wagons waited outside the Shop, piled high and ready to go. Indoors, all still buzzed with final preparations. Packs were being adjusted, ropes tightened, inventories checked. For a moment no one noticed the three figures who lurched in from outside.

Then Runa's hood fell aside. Her pale, grubby face could be seen. Someone seized her as her legs gave way and she slipped from Jandilay's arms.

"It's the Princess!"

"Princess Runa!"

"Your Highness!"

The room erupted. Everyone rushed to welcome the thin, stooped figure, to find her a chair, to bring her food and drink, to hold her begrimed hands, to wipe the dirt from her face. A lost hero had been found and they gathered her into their midst.

Jandilay stepped aside, not sorry to be forgotten. This, he thought, was what it all meant: the care these people had for each other, Wheeler and human alike. This was the standard he himself must now live up to. And it was into this fellowship that he must bring Onna Val, whether she wanted to come or not. How long did he have before the wagons set out? An hour? Two at most? He hurried out into the night and back the way he'd come.

CHAPTER TWENTY-ONE

A WARM NIGHT IN THE KITCHENS

Slipping back into the palace was easy. Finding the way from the secret door was not. Jandilay quickly got lost and wasted valuable time getting his bearings. As the minutes ticked by, his heart beat faster and faster. He couldn't let Halvan and the Mongos leave without him and Onna Val!

Firelight danced on the walls ahead. Someone was awake. Shouting could be heard. At the same time, a smell of fresh bread reached his nostrils. The kitchens! This must be where Eviret was preparing her Magic Egg! Onna Val would be there. Throwing caution to the winds, Jandilay ran down the hall, around a corner, and straight into the noise and glare.

The first person he saw was Captain Evington. Two guards held him fast.

"I want my share!" he screamed, struggling and twisting in their arms. "You promised me my share! Give it to me now!"

Chefs and kitchen maids cowered against walls or behind ovens and shelves, their eyes wide with fear. If a dragon had burst up through the floor, breathing fire and death, they could hardly have been more terrified. Onna Val stood wringing her hands, her panicked eyes darting back and forth between Evington and a solitary figure in the center of the room.

It took a moment for Jandilay to realize that this solitary figure was the Queen Regent. He barely recognized her. Her lovely hair hung in wet tendrils around her head and shoulders. Her face gleamed with sweat. Great patches of flour and grease streaked her gown. And to complete the bizarre picture, she was frantically cramming something into her mouth—something brown and bready. Her wide-open mouth was already so full that she could barely chew and her cheeks puffed out like balloons. She gave a huge swallow, almost choked on it, got it down by main force, and kept grinding away at the rest.

Onna Val darted over to Jandilay. "I'm so glad you're here!" she cried. "It's been horrible!"

"Why? What happened?"

It had all gone well enough at first, Onna Val said. The cooks had begun a small batch of dough. When Eviret had broken the Magic Egg into it, the mixing bowl had glowed for a moment like a small sun, radiantly golden. Eviret had taken this as a good omen; the chefs had not. It was too much egg for such a small amount of pastry, they'd said, and couldn't possibly work unless they made a larger batch. Eviret would hear of no delay. She had seized the mixing bowl, stirred the Egg into the dough, then dumped it all out onto the counter. The chefs had ranted on and on about layers and butter, but to no avail. Eviret had taken over the operation and would listen to no one.

Soon she had wrestled the ingredients into a gray, blobby mass that everyone else regarded with dismay. Into the oven it had gone. After twenty anxious minutes (which might have been fifteen if Eviret hadn't kept opening the oven door) it had come out predictably flat, limp, and misshapen. An undaunted Evington had stood ready with a knife. "Equal shares," he had said, and bent down to do the slicing. It was this rash act that had precipitated his arrest and the Queen Regent's subsequent feeding frenzy.

"I think I've made an awful mistake!" Onna Val moaned. "Look at Eviret! She doesn't deserve a Magic Egg, does she?"

Jandilay agreed wholeheartedly. The last of the bread had just disappeared into Eviret's mouth (over Evington's strenuous objections). She was chewing doggedly, her face red and clenched. She swallowed some more, chewed some more, chewed and swallowed, chewed and swallowed. When at last she came to the end of it, she stood gasping and panting like a marathon runner. Her hands hung open in front of her, opening and closing on empty air. Everyone waited to see what she would do.

"I feel it!" she breathed in a voice of awe, pressing a greasy hand to her chest. "I feel it inside me. I've done it!" She raised her face to the ceiling and flung out her arms. "I'm immortal!" she cried out. "I will rule Ev forever!"

But all was not well. "Who said that?" she snarled, turning violently.

"Who said what?" asked Evington.

The Queen Regent seemed not to hear him. "Who said that?" she snarled again, wheeling from side to side. "Who said that? Show yourself! Come out where I can see you! Say it to my face, you cowards!"

They all looked at one another. They had heard nothing.

Eviret seemed to realize this. She saw for herself that no one else was speaking. No one else could hear what she apparently heard.

The meaning of this slowly dawned on her. "I know what's happened," she whispered. "It's what I've *longed* for. I hear your *thoughts!* Yes, it's true! The nasty, mean, ungrateful thoughts that fill your heads—I hear them *all.* How *wonderful!* You will never have secrets from me again."

This struck no one as a good thing. Several kitchen maids fell to the floor in horror. Others clapped their hands over their mouths as if they could somehow silence their rebellious thoughts. Eviret uttered her coarse, braying laugh.

Then that laugh turned into to a wail. "But you all *hate* me!" she moaned. "You're *afraid* of me, every one of you. You think I'm—oh, you think I'm a *tyrant!* It's so *unfair.* And it's so *loud!*" She pressed her hands to her temples as if they hurt her. "It's *too* loud! There are too *many* of you. I can't make it *out.* Can't you be *quiet,* you horrible people? Let me *think,* for pity's sake!" She lurched forward against one of the chefs. He tried to pull away, but she seized his apron and held fast.

Oddly, this seemed to clear her head. She stared up at the frightened man.

"You think I'm *insane!*" she whimpered. "Why, you treacherous little *beast!* And after everything I've *done* for you. I'll have you in *prison!*"

She pushed him away and tumbled back against Evington. If this physical contact somehow clarified her strange new faculties, it nevertheless brought her no comfort. "Uncle Evington, you want to *murder* me!" she screamed. "You're planning it right *now!* You want to take the throne for *yourself!* How *can* you? What have I ever done to *you?*"

Again she pushed away from the touch that tormented her. By sheer bad luck she tumbled straight into Jandilay. Both crashed to the floor in a tangle of arms, legs, and hair.

Eviret recovered first. She stared down at the startled Jandilay. A shaky smile spread across her damp, blotchy face. "Why, it's you! My friend from An. Or is it Oz? Well, what does it matter? You don't hate me, do you? You're kind and good, and—oh!" Her smile vanished. "Oh! You—you *traitor!* You *creature!* And Halvan. *Halvan!* And the people from the theater. They're trying to—no! They're trying to get the Wheelers out of the *city.* In *wagons.* I see it in your mind. They're on their way to the gates this very *minute.* This is Runa's *plot!* And Runa is *there.* You've rescued her from prison *right under my very nose!*"

She scrambled to her feet.

"Evington!" she shouted. "This is your chance to redeem yourself. Take your men to the city gates. Do you hear me? You've got to stop those wagons! Stop them immediately! Not one must get out of the city!"

"What about the people on them?" quavered Evington, trying to sound brave and bold.

"Throw them all into the dungeons, along with my wretched sister! Take this one, too." She seized Jandilay's collar and flung him at Evington. No one else moved. "As for you," she went on, turning to Onna Val. "You've got a flying cloud, I hear? Very well. I want my father and I want him *now*. Take me to the Red Castle—or your friends will all meet a *very* unpleasant end indeed!"

CHAPTER TWENTY-TWO

THE RED CASTLE

here's one thing I don't understand," Ojo said as they flew. "Jinnicky is a powerful wizard. He can do practically anything. Why hasn't he broken Evardo's enchantment?"

It was mid-afternoon and Bud and Fluff were making their first journey as swallows, courtesy of Button-Bright's Yookoohoo powers. The Red Castle was their destination. They had started with a northerly detour alongside the mountains and then turned toward the Nonestic coast, where the mountains dwindled to a more manageable size. This made the return journey far pleasanter than the rougher route the boys had used yesterday.

"Ojo, we've spent the last two years asking ourselves that question," said Fluff. "Jinnicky refuses to explain. He says the cure will come to him when it's ready, and until then there's nothing he can do."

"Do you believe him?"

"Evanna doesn't," said Bud. "She's Evardo's sister. She swore she'd camp out on Jinnicky's doorstep till he did something useful. As far as we know she's still there."

"I don't know what to think," said Fluff. "Jinnicky loves Evardo. He's thrilled that a king of Ev actually wants to be friends with him. None of them ever did before, so it was a big relief when they finally met. After that we used to spend our vacations at the Red Castle. Even the two girls went with us. Now—oh, I wish I understood!"

When they saw the vast expanse of ocean in front of them they turned eastward into Ix. Fishing villages could be seen below, and later a great bay with a thriving harbor city. All this was Queen Zixi's realm. A great deal of shipping went back and forth between Ix and Noland, Bud said. To the two boys, who had spent most of their lives in a landlocked country, the majestic sailing ships presented an entrancing spectacle. "We've got to come back here," they agreed. Beyond this bay the country grew wilder, though farmlands could be glimpsed far inland. Pristine beaches streamed away beneath. It looked like wonderful country for a holiday. Out to sea they glimpsed two islands, one of which Bud said was called Nonagon Island.

The westering sun lay directly behind when their destination finally emerged from the glare. As they approached, Ojo and Button-Bright got their first close look at the Red Jinn's remarkable realm.

"It's not just one castle," said Ojo wonderingly. "It's a whole city of little castles with a big castle right in the middle."

And so it was. All around the big central castle, with its one hundred front steps, lay dozens of perfect little copies. Nor was this the only unique thing about them. All had been built of red glass that the sunset made even redder. Red kaleidoscopes spun and glittered in every roof and turret, and the walls were lavishly set with rubies. It dazzled the bright black eyes of the swallows. To Ojo and Button-Bright it looked even redder and more ruby-studded than Glinda's red palace in the Quadling Country.

"Jinnicky is the master here," said Fluff. "But he makes sure every little castle has its own king. They seem to like it that way."

"There's someone sitting on the palace steps," said Button-Bright. "Look."

He was right. At the very top of the steps sat an elderly woman dressed in Evite fashion. She wore no headdress, and the evening breeze blew her short gray curls about her face. She was watching the sun-reddened clouds with a sad expression.

"Evanna!" called Fluff. She flew down and alighted, closely followed by the others.

The woman rose in alarm. "Who are you?" she asked. "How do you know my name?"

Fluff quickly told her. She also introduced her companions and explained why they had come there in the forms of swallows.

The woman seemed to calm down at once. "I certainly know King Bud and Queen Fluff," she said with a smile, "though you don't look much like yourself in these fine feathers. As for your two friends, I honor anyone from the

Land of Oz—especially if they come bearing magic. Let me introduce myself. I am Evanna, eldest daughter of Evoldo the Mad and eldest sister of King Evardo."

The boys greeted her politely, bowing their feathered heads.

Fluff hopped up onto Evanna's shoulder. "I'm sorry I've been gone so long," she said. "You'd think I'd been asleep myself. It took Ojo and Button-Bright to wake me up. Have there been any changes here?"

"Changes in this place? Not likely. King Evardo still sleeps and the Red Jinn still refuses to do anything about it. Oh, there is one change. Jinnicky has banned me from the castle. He says he's tired of my constant complaining. Well, he has a point. I never give him a moment's peace—or didn't till he shut me out. Nowadays his people keep me fed and housed and that's all. But here I am all the same. I don't give up."

Evanna had a brisk, no-nonsense quality that the boys warmed to. At the same time, they could imagine what she would be like if her temper were roused.

"Will the Red Jinn see us, do you think?" asked Fluff.

Evanna laughed. "He might. Fresh faces perk him up, I've noticed. It's only my old face that irritates him. Go on in and I'll follow behind."

The four swallows found Jinnicky's throne room as splendid as its exterior promised. On both sides huge glass pillars alternated with beautifully fashioned glass vases, all as red as the ruby throne that sat high on a dais at the end of the hall.

"No one's here," said Button-Bright, alighting below the throne.

"Don't be too sure," said Bud, fluttering down beside him. Their swallow feet scraped across the glass floor. "When our friend the Red Jinn is napping he can be hard to find."

Certainly there was no lack of hiding places. Amid the splendor the swallows saw a vast and varied clutter of bags, baskets, and boxes. Some overflowed with rubies, but most contained other things: bottles and jars filled with magical potions and powders, as well as magical implements of every kind. A large red umbrella reminded Button-Bright of his own Magic Umbrella, now lost forever. Off to one side stood the Red Jinn's famous jinrikisha. The only thing missing was the Red Jinn himself.

"Button-Bright," said Fluff. "Are you planning to change us back at some point?"

The boy gave a laugh. "Oh, sorry! I forgot about that. Ojo and I sometimes go all day without ever being human. Here you go." As quick as thought he restored all four swallows to their natural forms.

"My mercy me!" someone shouted.

"Blasts and blizzards!
Some wizard or wizards
Have come to settle

CHAPTER TWENTY-TWO

My wizardly gizzard!"

Out from under the jinrikisha rolled a large red jug. Two stubby arms heaved it up onto two equally stubby legs. Off popped the lid. Underneath was the unmistakable face of the Red Jinn, a stout old fellow with red whiskers and long red hair. In addition to his jug he ordinarily wore a jolly expression, but just now he appeared thoroughly alarmed. He dashed about the room as if he were looking for something or someone.

"Where's that Wizard?" Jinnicky fumed. "I know he's here somewhere. Nobody else would barge right into my castle with all this foreign magic!"

"Jinnicky, Jinnicky!" cried Fluff. "There's no foreign wizard here. It's just us."

Jinnicky pulled up short and stared at his visitors. A huge grin lit up his round face. "Why, so it is!" he exclaimed. "What a grand, glorious, gleesome surprise! Welcome, welcome!" They couldn't help laughing as he merrily shook each of their hands in turn. "My dear Fluff! It's been much too long. You're lovelier than ever. And is this your brother, all the way from Noland? Delighted, delighted. Oh, Evanna. Still hanging around, I see. Don't you ever stop? And what's this? Two boys from Oz or I'm a ziggamaroon! Let me see, it's—no, don't tell me. Button-Jo and Obright?"

He knew perfectly well what their real names were. They had a good laugh over it.

"Good, we're all friends now," Evanna said briskly. Getting down to business—"

"But seriously," Jinnicky interrupted, peering behind the group. "Somebody just wizzed a few wizzes, didn't they? Four birds turned into four people. You can't tell me that's red magic. That's Oz magic. Is the Wizard of Oz hiding in somebody's pants pocket?"

The answer to this question caught him by surprise. Last time Jinnicky had seen the two boys, they'd had no more magic than most other people. Now, he was told, Button-Bright had discovered a talent for transformation and Ojo was doing his best to cope with a Magic Egg. Jinnicky shook his head so hard that his lid rattled.

"There's far too much magic in Oz," he sighed. "Witches, giants, and now boys. Who can keep track of it all? Ev magic is right here where it belongs, in my own castle. Are you sure this magic of yours isn't wizard magic?" They were sure. "And I'm still the mighty master of red magic?" They willingly confirmed that he was. "Then I suppose I'll have to put up with it. Truffles and tarts, but I'm pleased to see all of you!"

"We're pleased to see you too," grinned Bud. "Still, this isn't a social call."

"That's true," said Evanna. "The fact is—"

"Wait!" shouted Jinnicky, springing to his feet. He raced to his throne, seized a small silver bell, and rang it vigorously. At once a smiling boy in a huge turban appeared beside him. "Dinner for my guests!" the Jinn commanded. "And Ginger, make it a real whomperoo of a feast—the best we've got."

Ginger—for indeed this was the Red Jinn's most famous servant—vanished at once. Half a second later he reappeared with a table set for six, as well as six chairs. Then he disappeared again, only to reappear with a covered tray, which he placed on the table. Five more times he disappeared, and five more times he reappeared with yet another tray. This seemed to complete his duties. With a final wink he was gone.

"Now, Jinnicky—" began Evanna.

"Fall to!" roared the Jinn, cutting her off.

"Hungry is what travelers are,

Whether they come from near or far.

So eat, eat, eat—with a har, har, har!"

Ojo had the feeling that all this was a distraction. For reasons of his own, the Red Jinn didn't want to get down to business. Still, it really was dinner time and they'd flown a long way. All sat down and shook out their napkins.

Fluff tried to stay on track. "It's true we're hungry," she conceded. "And we appreciate the hospitality. But as Evanna was saying a minute ago—"

"Look what Ginger's done!" interrupted the Jinn. "He's a genius, I tell you, a Ginger of a genius. Each of us has a different dinner, and rubies to rivets we've all got our own particular favorites. Am I right?"

They took the covers off their trays.

"Mushroom pot pie," said Bud. "Yes, that's my favorite all right."

"I've got squash soup and potato salad," said Ojo. "How did Ginger know?"

Fluff had a lovely soufflé that smelled marvelous. Even Evanna eyed her black beans and rice with deep satisfaction. As for Button-Bright, he found a little bit of everything on his tray. Ojo chuckled at this.

"Perfect!" the Munchkin boy said. "Button-Bright never can decide what his favorite is."

"That's Ojo's way of saying I'll eat whatever's in front of me," said Button-Bright.

They had to admit that Ginger had somehow whipped up a perfect dinner. Jinnicky watched proudly as they dug into it. "There's nothing like red magic for getting you just what you wish for most," he declared.

"Is that so?" said Evanna, setting down a forkful of black beans. "Then let me tell you what I wish. It's been three years since—"

There was a huge crash as Jinnicky's chair tumbled over backward. He had pushed off from the table with his short, stubby arms and now lay on the floor with his short, stubby fingers in his ears. His guests looked at him in astonishment. "Alibabble!" he yelled. "Alibabble, come in here this minute!"

A tall, turbaned figure stalked into the room and glared down at the prostrate Jinn. He had a noble nose and a stern expression.

"Alibabble, you're my Grand Advizier," Jinnicky said from his prone posture. "Well, I need some Grand Advizing right now! What do you do when somebody keeps trying to tell you something you already know and you wish you didn't?"

"That's the least of your worries," Alibabble replied. "First things first."

Jinnicky sat up. "What do you mean by that, you old parrotpuss?"

"Important guests are seeing you in a deplorable state. Your throne room is a mess. You haven't polished your jar lately. Worst of all, your hair has gotten much too long again. Mend these mishaps and then we will speak of your other concerns."

Jinnicky's face turned as red as his palace. He opened his mouth to protest. What he might have said remained unknown, however, for Fluff leaped to her feet.

"This has got to stop!" she exploded. She strode around the table and loomed over the startled Jinn. "So you already know what I'm going to say, do you? Good for you. It doesn't take red magic to figure that out. I want my husband back and I want him awake! Now what are you going to do about it?"

"Nothing!" shrieked the Jinn. "There's nothing I *can* do! It's out of my hands!"

"So you keep saying," scolded Evanna. "But you've yet to tell us why."

"I want to see my husband!" Fluff insisted. "Where are you keeping him?"

"It's a reasonable request," Alibabble said calmly. "The lady is his wife, after all."

Jinnicky gave a long wail. Then he collapsed into a heap of utter frustration. "You can see him," he said. "And much good may it do you."

CHAPTER TWENTY-THREE

RED MAGIC

ow that he'd made up his mind, the Red Jinn wasted no time. He scrambled to his feet and hurried toward what looked like a random pile of objects. From this he pulled a small chest of drawers. The visitors watched him in bewilderment. Pretty though the thing might be, with its cunning pattern of small rubies, it couldn't have been bigger than a hat box. What did it have to do with the sleeping King of Ev? Jinnicky lugged it to a clear space in the middle of the room and beckoned the others to gather around it.

"My friend Evardo is as safe as can be," he said. "Observe."

He turned the knob on the middle drawer—left, right, and left again, as if it were a combination lock. A loud click was heard. The middle drawer floated right out of the chest and hung suspended in the air, where it slowly revolved once, twice, three times. Finally, with a small *flumpf*, it transformed itself into a full-size bed.

"Evardo!" cried Fluff, and rushed to the bedside. For there, sleeping peacefully, lay the old king himself.

He was tall and handsome, with silver hair and a silver beard to match. His clothing was rich yet simple: a tunic of purple velvet, a slim golden belt, and black leggings. His hands, clasped on his chest, rose and fell with the rhythm of his breathing. Ojo thought he looked wise and kind. Fluff tenderly kissed his cheek and stroked his brow.

"My love," she said. "I'm here. I haven't forgotten. Oh, won't you come back to me?"

Evanna leaned over him too. The sleeper did not stir. His eyes remained closed and his spirit walked in the mysterious dreams of its enchantment.

Ojo's heart went out to the King's grieving Queen and faithful sister. He remembered the sorrow he had felt when his own Unc Nunkie fell under a spell of petrefaction. Unc's spell had been broken in a matter of weeks, while Evardo's had now lasted three years. How had Fluff and Evanna borne this ordeal so patiently? Ojo knelt beside them. "May I try?" he asked.

"May you try what?" said an aggrieved voice behind him. It was the Red Jinn.

"To wake up the King," Ojo replied.

"Ojo can do amazing things," said Button-Bright. "It's the Magic Egg inside him."

"This enchantment has nothing to do with your Magic Eggs!" Jinnicky argued. "I tell you it's no good."

Fluff turned on Jinnicky. "How do you know it's no good? You didn't cast the spell, did you? It's not your kind of magic."

"No. Yes. That is—I didn't cast the spell. But it's—oh, just leave it, can't you?"

"I don't want to leave it," Fluff said stubbornly. "If Ojo thinks he can help, I say we should let him try."

Jinnicky flung out his fat hands as if in befuddlement at the unaccountable ways of the world. "Well, *I* want no part of it. Wake me when you've realized it's hopeless." With that he withdrew into his jar. The lid came down with a thud.

Ojo did not like to annoy their host. When he looked down at the sleeping King, though, he knew he must go through with it. "Jinnicky may be right," he said uncomfortably. "Fluff, you shouldn't get your hopes up." He placed his boyish hands on Evardo's chest, not sure whether anything would happen at all. At once he felt the presence of powerful magic just out of reach. It filled the King with its own invisible intent and pushed at Ojo's fingers as if it didn't want to let him in. He pushed back, testing its strength. There was no give to it. He pushed still harder—not with his hands but with the power inside him, the sunlit core that so often helped him in moments of need. He trembled. A vivid impression of scarlet suffused his mind. He pulled his hands back.

"It's red magic," he said.

"Red magic?" said Bud. "What do you mean?"

"The enchantment. It's red magic—the magic of the Red Castle."

Fluff stared at him. "That's impossible," she said. "Evardo was nowhere near here when he fell asleep. It happened at home in Evna."

"I don't know about that," said Ojo. "I just know this is red magic through and through. It's the reddest magic I ever heard of. It's protecting your husband, Fluff, but it's also what's keeping him asleep."

Bud placed a hand on Ojo's shoulder. "Red magic means Jinnicky," he said soberly. "Ojo, if this is true—"

CHAPTER TWENTY-THREE

A growling sound interrupted him. They all looked at Jinnicky's jar.

The thing was rocking like a dinghy on rough waters. Out of it came a rumble that grew louder and louder every second. Jinnicky's arms and legs burst forth suddenly, followed by his head. "I told you it was no good!" the frantic Jinn shouted at Ojo. "But did you listen? No! You had to go poking and prying around with your exhausting, exasperous, exaggerific Egg magic. And now look what's happened! Everyone thinks *I* cast this spell!" He dove headlong into a pile of detritus and came up again with a small box clutched in his fat fist. "Do you see this?" he shouted, waving it at his guests. "Do you see what's in here?"

The boxtop flapped wildly. What lay beneath was plain to see.

"It's empty," said Button-Bright.

"Precisely!" moaned Jinnicky, flinging the box away. "Empty, blank, bleak. It used to be full of red magic and now it's empty. Somebody stole this spell!" He pulled his lid down hard upon his head. He was hugely embarrassed.

"I begin to understand," said Evanna. "Let me guess, Jinnicky. The spell in this box was a sleeping spell?" The lid wagged up and down woefully. "And it disappeared, oh, about three years ago?"

"No!" yelled the Jinn. "Maybe. I don't know. It could have disappeared sometime before that. I can't tell you when because I don't check every bit of my magic every day, or even every year. I trust my people. Somebody from somewhere else stole it, somebody with a scurvy, scrofulous, scalawagonizing scheme. And that somebody used it on my poor friend Evardo! It's a disastrophe! If only I'd listened to Alibabble and kept this place tidier, none of this would have happened." Jinnicky gave a howl of grief. Fluff seized the poor fellow's hands.

"And this is why you can't break the spell?"

He nodded miserably. "It's my own spell. I know how it works. I also know the one thing that can break it. And I absolutely, definitively cannot tell you what that one thing is." He flung himself down on the floor.

"Why on earth would you make a spell that way?" asked Button-Bright.

"I thought no one would use it but me! How was I to know it would be stolen?"

"My dear Jinnicky," said Fluff. "Couldn't you have explained this three years ago?"

"I was ashamed," he said, hanging his head so that only the top of his lid could be seen. "Wouldn't you be?"

"I *am* ashamed," said Fluff.

Jinnicky looked up at her. "You, my dear? But why?"

"Because it's obvious who must have stolen the spell. It was my own dear daughter Eviret. Evardo and I raised her. It's our fault that she turned out this way."

Bud shook his head. "Fluff, you know better than that. You and Evardo did your best with your daughter. Now that she's all grown up, she can take responsibility for her own actions. And if I'm right, we may get the chance to tell her so. Jinnicky, we have reason to believe Eviret is on her way here to collect her father."

Jinnicky sprang to attention. "Really?"

"That's right," said Ojo. "With magic from her very own Magic Egg."

If they thought this would alarm the Red Jinn, they were wrong. He uttered an ecstatic whoop. Then he capered about the room. Evanna watched with growing irritation till he came to a standstill, grinning delightedly. "That's that, then," he said. "We might as well sit back down to dinner because there's no more to be done tonight."

"No more to be done?" echoed Evanna. "Didn't you hear what Bud and Ojo just said? Eviret is coming here, and it's not just to be neighborly. She means to see to it that her father never wakes up. Is that what you want?"

"Yes!" crowed Jinnicky with a bound into the air. "The cure is finally coming to us!"

CHAPTER
TWENTY-FOUR

THE BIGGEST
DIPLOMATIC MESS
EVER

innicky did his utmost to keep everyone entertained. Dinner was followed by a sumptuous array of cakes, puddings and pies, each more delicious than the last. When these had been polished off he got out his famous band box. Fluff, Bud, and Evanna had seen the band box before, but the boys from Oz had never known anything like the crackerjack band that marched out in full uniform and launched into a rollicking number. Invited in from the city outside, Jinnicky's people spent the evening dancing to one tune after another while their turbans swayed on their heads.

"You don't suppose Jinnicky is still trying to distract us, do you?" Button-Bright said privately to Ojo. The air had been cleared somewhat, and nobody blamed the little Jinn for

Eviret's use of his spell. But why had he kicked up his heels so gleefully at the news that Eviret was descending upon them with goodness knows what terrible new powers? Jinnicky refused to say. This did little to assuage the fears of Evanna and the Nolanders. Their faith was wavering and all the music and good cheer in the world couldn't conceal it.

At last it was time to say good night. Bud and Fluff accepted Evanna's invitation to stay with her in the small castle she'd been living in for the past three years. Jinnicky watched sadly while they walked off down the hundred front steps.

"They're not happy with me," he said.

"Do you blame them?" asked Ojo. "Why won't you tell them what you're going to do?"

"Because I can't!" Jinnicky sighed. "You may think I don't know my red magic from my yellow magic, but I truly do. I have a real whizbanger of a plan! It will look like a betrayal to them and they'll try to stop me. At least I hope they will. If they don't, the plan won't be such a whizbanger after all."

"Jinnicky," said Button-Bright, "that's nonsense."

Jinnicky gave a half-hearted har-har. "It *looks* like nonsense," he admitted. "But it's the only hope for my poor friend Evardo. You two have to help me with it."

"Us? What can we do?"

"Something you'll absolutely, utterly, and completely hate doing. In fact, we'll all have to do something we hate— especially me. I'll have to do the most excruciable thing I've ever done in my life. I can't tell you what it is, but believe me, I'll hate it. So will you. As for our three friends down there, they'll go right through the roof. They'll put up a huge, horrificacious fuss and try to stop me. Now, that's very important. They have to want to stop me, and we have to let them try. *Try*, mind you. Not succeed, just give it a good honest whack. That's where you come in. You have to stop them from stopping me."

Ojo's heart sank. This particular job had his name written all over it. "That's your plan? You want me to turn my magic on our friends?" The Red Jinn nodded. "Well, you were right in one way," Ojo said. "I hate everything about it."

"Me too!" said Button-Bright. "Why, it'll look as if we're in league with Eviret. Jinnicky, can't you at least tell *us* what will happen?"

The Red Jinn couldn't and wouldn't. All would turn out for the best, he avowed, if they only trusted him. He seemed so desperately confident, so sure that this was what Evardo needed, that at last the boys shook on it. Privately, they hoped they wouldn't live to regret the bargain.

They were given a little bedroom overlooking the garden. After Jinnicky left, though, they couldn't manage to settle down. The events of the past few days weighed on them, and so did the knowledge of what was coming. Even worse, they didn't know how long they'd have to wait till the next shoe dropped. "Nothing is going the way it was supposed to when we started out," sighed Ojo. "We've already made one big mistake."

"Believing Eviret," said Button-Bright. "Yes, that was a mistake all right."

"So how do we know this isn't an even bigger mistake? No matter what we do, it could all go wrong!"

"For a lot of people besides us," said Button-Bright. "King Evardo, Bud and Fluff, the Wheelers, even Halvan. Not to mention Jandilay and Onna Val! It's the biggest diplomatic mess ever. And you know what else? None of it has anything to do with our real problem, which is Dame Zanket."

"That's right! We never asked Bud about Dame Zanket. How could we forget?"

"There's just too much to worry about."

"Much too much. I wish we were at home in Gugu Forest right now."

"So do I!"

This got both of them thinking, and their thoughts led them to the same conclusion. How much better it would be if they slept outside, as they'd grown accustomed to doing! Fresh sea air would be just the thing. So Button-Bright turned them both back into swallows and they made themselves comfortable on a branch just outside their window. The sound of ocean waves lulled them to sleep.

CHAPTER TWENTY-FIVE

TREACHERY OR TRIUMPH?

"OJO! Ojo, wake up!"

Ojo opened his eyes and gave his feathers a shake. Gray twilight veiled the sky above him. Where was he? Gugu Forest, as he'd been dreaming a moment ago? No. Drained of all color in this eerie dusk, the walls and turrets of the Red Castle loomed just yards away.

"What time is it?" he asked sleepily.

"The sun's not up yet," whispered Button-Bright, perched close beside him on their tree branch. "But somebody else is. Listen."

Ojo listened. A shrill voice floated over the top of the castle.

"What is that? You don't suppose it's—"

"Yes I do. She's already here. Come on, let's see what's happening! Quietly, though. It might be better if nobody notices us for a while."

Ojo agreed. Considering the promise they'd made to Jinnicky last night, and what he knew he'd have to do as a result, he very much preferred to remain incognito. How else could he bear the expression on poor Fluff's face? He only hoped the Red Jinn's plan (whatever it was) would turn out well for all of them. The two swallows shook off their drowsiness and soared up into the air.

The ruckus seemed to be coming from the front of the castle. When they got there, a strange sight met their eyes.

Just above the front steps hovered a small cloud. It had to be Onna Val's, Ojo thought. And there the girl was, crouching uneasily to one side. But who was the dangerous lunatic teetering in the middle of the cloud? At first all they saw through the gray light was a wet, tangled mass of hair and a gown that looked as if it had been soaked in grease and then dragged through a chalk quarry. Surely the Eviret they knew would not allow herself to be seen this way. Yet Eviret it was, flaunting her disarray before a growing crowd of Jinnicky's people. Like Button-Bright and Ojo, the sleepy miners had been wakened by the shouting and now stood in a curious huddle at the bottom of the steps. More arrived every minute.

"I want to see your master!" Eviret demanded. "Bring him out here *right now!*"

Alibabble stood in the castle doorway. "Madame," he said icily, "might I suggest the services of a barber and a laundress instead? Come down off that cloud and I'll see what we can arrange for you."

The miners tittered.

"Oh!" screamed Eviret. "You'll pay for that, you *lackey!* I want the Red *Jinn!*"

"And here he is," said Jinnicky himself, stepping out from behind his Grand Advizier. "Alibabble, I'll take it from here. Go get yourself some breakfast if you're hungry. Or if you'd rather, you can stay and enjoy the show." Alibabble had no intention of missing a single minute. He posted himself behind his master and watched with interest. So did the miners. As for the two swallow-boys, they concealed themselves in a bit of shrubbery alongside the steps.

"Now," said Jinnicky, facing the wild-haired Queen Regent. "Since we already know each other, my dear Eviret, I think we can get down to it. You're here for your father."

Eviret did not answer at once. Indeed, she appeared to be in some sort of difficulty. She reeled dangerously and pressed her hands to her temples. "Be *quiet*, will you?" she hissed at Onna Val. "How can I hear *myself* thinking over what *you're* thinking?"

"Onna Val didn't say anything," Ojo whispered to Button-Bright. "Did she?"

Button-Bright shook his head. Far from interrupting, Onna Val appeared to be watching in a state of real fear. What had happened to her?

Eviret collected herself sufficiently to answer the Red Jinn. "I *do* want my father," she said with a vain attempt at dignity. "But how on earth did *you* know it?"

"Har har har!" laughed Jinnicky. "I've been expecting this visit for two years! My only question is what took you so long. This whole miserable, magnominious mess could have been cleared up ages ago. But here you are at last, and guess what? I'm going to give you exactly what you want."

This sounded ominous. "He doesn't mean that, does he?" Ojo whispered.

Eviret also doubted the Red Jinn's sincerity. "I don't understand," she said. "Do you mean to say you'll *give* my father to me? Freely and without condition?"

"Almost," said Jinnicky. "I do have one small condition—"

"Stop, stop, stop!" cried a voice of outrage. Three figures burst through the crowd of miners and swarmed up the steps. In the growing light, Ojo saw that they were Evanna, Bud, and Fluff. Up until now he'd been hoping they would stay away altogether, but the noise had wakened them along with everyone else. All three had clearly just tumbled out of bed. Fluff's hair floated loose about her shoulders, and both she and Evanna wore nightgowns. Bud had on a pair of pajamas and a confused expression.

Evanna led the charge. "This can't be true!" she cried from just behind Onna Val's cloud. "Jinnicky, tell me you did *not* just promise to give my brother to this murderous usurper!"

"Did too!" shouted Jinnicky, jumping up and down in excitement. His lid bounced on his head. "And that's what's going to happen. What are you going to do about it?"

"Nothing!" screamed Eviret. Unsteadily, she turned to confront her relations. "Aunt Evanna, I am your ruler and I *forbid* you to interfere. I forbid you to *think* about interfering. I can hear you from here. I hear all of you! Get *away* from me with your horrible noisy thoughts! They make me want to *scream!*"

No one knew quite what to make of this. It was somebody else who explained.

"The Magic Egg changed her!" Onna Val called out. "She reads minds!"

"That's right," Eviret said triumphantly. "I know what every single *one* of you is thinking. You're all *furious*. You thought the Jinn was on *your* side and it turns out he's on *my* side. Poor you! And you all *hate* me—even my own precious mother! Well, stew in your own juices, Mother. You and Uncle Bud may be royalty in *Noland*, but in Ev *I'm* the Queen Regent. So get out of here and *leave me alone!*"

"Eviret, I don't hate you," said Fluff. "I just wish you'd behave like a decent, reasonable human being!"

"Where has Jinnicky gone?" Bud asked suddenly.

They all looked at the palace. Alibabble stood alone in the doorway.

"My master is busy," he said. "No, wait. Here he comes."

The Grand Advizier stepped away from the door. Out of it, to everyone's horror, floated King Evardo's bed—with King Evardo still asleep upon it. Onward it came, serene and steady, until it drifted to a halt just shy of Onna Val's cloud. After it came Jinnicky. His hands steered the airborne bed by means of magic.

Fluff cried out. Until this moment she hadn't believed that the little Jinn would betray her. The appearance of the bed dashed her hopes. "Jinnicky!" she pleaded. "I thought you were our friend. Please, please don't give Evardo to my daughter. Give him to me, give him to Evanna, or keep him yourself if you must. But don't let Eviret have him!"

"Evardo trusted you, Jinnicky," Bud said sternly. "And now he's helpless."

"*We're* not helpless!" stormed Evanna. "We'll take Evardo by force if we have to!"

Ojo braced himself. His moment had arrived. "Button-Bright!" he whispered. "Turn me into something tiny!"

At once he became a bee. He buzzed up out of their hiding place.

Eviret tried to plant her unsteady feet on the cloud. "I'm not afraid of you, Aunt Evanna," she sneered. "I'm not afraid of *anyone* anymore. I swallowed a Magic *Egg* last night. This girl here brought it to me from the Land of An— from the great Phoenix *himself!* She seems to regret it now, the ungrateful little *minx*, but at the time she was quite pleased with herself."

"It's all true," moaned Onna Val. "I'm so sorry! I didn't understand."

The Queen Regent only laughed. "As if anyone cares! The point is, *I* am now the possessor of mighty magic. I'm immortal at last! It's why I can read all your stupid, treacherous *minds*. *No* one can harm me. *No* one can oppose me. If you so much as *stir*, I will strike you down with my power!"

"We'll see about that!" growled Evanna. "Come on, Bud!" And with the Nolanders at her side, she made a dash at the floating bed.

Ojo's magic blazed within him—though to what end he did not know. He must keep his promise to Jinnicky. But how? Must he protect his friends from Eviret? Or must he protect Eviret from his friends? Or both? As sometimes happened in moments of danger, he felt time slow almost to a standstill. The surging figures of Evanna, Bud, and Fluff barely moved and a strange hush fell over the scene. Moreover, Ojo saw things he could not see at other times. He saw a core of magic burning in the breast of the Queen Regent, just where it burned in himself at this very moment. Yet her magic was not like his. It was bent and cramped. Instead of shining its light outward, it turned inward on itself. She raised her arms— slowly, slowly, as he himself had done so often—to stop her enemies. Nothing happened. She could not harm them or even hinder them, for her power refused to serve her. Ojo knew now how to keep his promise. He buzzed down before the hurrying figures and put forth his strength.

Time blazed back. A shimmering net of magic descended over Evanna, Bud, and Fluff. They beat on it helplessly. It held them fast.

Eviret could not see the tiny bee hovering below her and thought she'd done it herself.

"That is how I smite my enemies!" she shouted ecstatically, teetering on her perch. She resembled a tipsy teenager more than she did a smiter of enemies. "I will vanquish all who oppose me! I will rule Ev forever!"

"Quite right," beamed Jinnicky. He seemed thoroughly pleased with this development and paid no attention to the three friends struggling frantically within their magic net. He did, however, aim a sly wink at the hovering bee. "And now back to business. As I said a few moments ago, I have one condition before I release Evardo into your care."

"Name it!" Eviret said proudly. "But make it quick. I want to get back to Evna. There's a rebellion I need to deal with."

"Imagine that," said Jinnicky. "Now listen. A few years ago you took something from me. May I have it back?"

Eviret had not expected this. She hesitated, and the growing light caught a sudden blush on her grimy cheek. Or was it just a reflection from the Red Castle? "I don't know what you mean," she said fretfully. "I have nothing of yours."

"Nothing you remember, perhaps. Small loss then, wouldn't you say? So I ask you again: may I have this thing back in exchange for your father?"

The moment of truth, Ojo sensed, had arrived. Jinnicky's whole plan hinged on Eviret's answer. She looked down at the Jinn as if she were trying to read his mind and couldn't quite manage it. Was there a hidden catch? What had she forgotten?

"I tell you I don't have anything that belongs to you!"

"Then you won't miss it when it's gone. Say it's mine and you've got a deal."

"Oh, very well," she said at last. "The fact is I used to steal from you all the *time*. Whatever *particular* trash I took from you, I certainly don't want it anymore. It's yours! Now give me my father!"

"Done!" yelled Jinnicky, falling over backward in his glee.

At that moment the sun rose. Its rays fell upon the sleeping King. He stirred. He raised a hand to his forehead. He sat up.

King Evardo had awakened.

CHAPTER
TWENTY-SIX

BUTTON-BRIGHT
STEPS UP

So dawned a morning of laughter and tears.

Jinnicky provided much of the laughter. The success of his plan sent him right through his own red glass roof and, in addition, gave him much to explain. He repeated the tale of his triumph at every opportunity.

"I *didn't* know she'd be clairvoyant!" he declared in answer to Button-Bright's question. "Who could? But I did know Eviret. Even as a little girl she always suspected we were thinking bad thoughts about her. That's why the whole charade had to be real. Poor Fluff and Evanna and Bud had to believe I'd really and truly sold them out, for Eviret would have seen right through them if they hadn't."

CHAPTER TWENTY-SIX

"I still don't understand what broke the spell," said King Bud.

Jinnicky explained that too. The sleeping spell was his own, designed and created so that it could only be removed by the person who cast it. The notion that someone else might steal it simply hadn't occurred to him. Eviret had stolen the spell and cast it herself, which meant that she alone had the power to wake her sleeping father.

"She had to be tricked into giving that spell back," the Jinn said. "The words alone would do it, but getting her to say those words? What a brain-blithering botheroozle of a job that was! And the Magic Egg nearly spoiled everything. If it had given her any real power, she wouldn't have cared about my little conditions. No sirree! Thank goodness she's such a miserable baker."

Eviret herself shed a great many tears, especially when Ojo convinced her (and the rest) that mind-reading was the only power she'd gotten from her Magic Egg. She spent a fruitless half hour trying to smite people who stubbornly remained un-smitten. Then she burst into sobs. A time came when everyone stopped paying attention to her.

As for Evardo and Fluff, they provided both tears and laughter in equal measure. No sooner had Ojo freed Fluff from his magic net than she bounded straight into her bewildered husband's arms. Their joyful and loving reunion brought tears to every eye. Evardo, it turned out, knew nothing of what had had transpired, how he had come to be here, or why his family and friends were so excited. He did know that he was ravenously hungry and needed a huge breakfast. Everyone needed breakfast, in fact. Ginger had his hands full for quite some time. Over a cheese omelet and a waffle, the well-rested King of Ev learned much that he wanted to understand.

"Eviret," he said, wagging a finger at his disgraced daughter, "I'm not ready to retire and you had no business rushing me. Even worse than what you did to me, though, is what they say you've done to the poor Wheelers. Fluff, my dear, there will be many ills to mend when we get home. Meanwhile, I have so many people to thank for my deliverance—Evites, Ozites, Nolanders, even a girl from the Land of An!"

Onna Val blushed. "I almost ruined everything," she said. "And the strange part is, I usually can't stand people like Eviret—big talkers who don't care about anybody else. They drive me crazy. Why did I fall for her story?"

"You did it because you love Jandilay," said Ojo.

"True," the girl sighed. "My one thought was getting him a good home. Oh! Jandilay!" She leaped to her feet. "I almost forgot. We can't sit here eating. We have to get back to Evna this very minute!"

"Why?" asked Evardo, instantly alarmed. "What happened?"

"The Wheelers are escaping with the theater people. Eviret found out about it. She left orders for the army to round them up and put them all into dungeons. Jandilay too."

"And Runa's in the dungeon already!" cried Fluff. "We have to get back!"

It was at this point that Evardo took command. Leaving a half-finished breakfast behind him, he marshalled every available means of transport. He and Fluff joined Onna Val on her traveling cloud. Bud and Evanna secured a ride in the Red Jinn's flying jinrikisha. Button-Bright and Ojo soared aloft as swallows. Only the wretched Eviret remained behind, in the tender care of Alibabble.

"At least she'll get a good haircut," Jinnicky chuckled. "Alibabble will see to that."

Soon the entire company was airborne and racing toward Evna.

As they approached the city, however, they were pulled up short by a surprising sight on the highway below. A long caravan wended its way out of the south. There were at least eight wagons, all pulled by teams of Wheelers and humans working in tandem.

"It's the theater people!" cried Onna Val. "They're not in prison!"

"Take us down!" commanded Evardo.

Down they all glided. Frightened faces turned skyward and a clamor of voices was heard. Fearing that the Queen

Regent had found them, the frightened refugees scurried to defend themselves—with a determined Princess Runa at their head. No one would take her friends to prison without a fight! But as soon as Runa saw her beloved father stepping down onto the ground, awake and full of joy, she raised a mighty cheer. All crowded around to welcome the restored monarch and his happy queen. Evardo couldn't stop embracing his joyful daughter.

"My poor Runa. What an awful time you've had. Fluff and I will look after you ourselves," the King told her.

To the Mongo brothers he said, "Of course you'll have your old posts back. Ridj, the palace can't run without you. And Drax, I hope to goodness you'll put every single Wheeler farce into storage. Let's have some real plays!"

The two brothers thanked him with all their hearts. Halvan threw his cap into the air.

"I'm an assistant again!" the ex-director cried. "Hurrah!"

"How did you escape?" Onna Val asked them. "Evington was on his way to arrest you."

"So he was," said Ridj. "But for once in his life he made his own decision. Didn't you, Evington old boy?"

At the Wheeler's shoulder stood Evington himself, looking confused and sheepish. "I did. It was the only thing to do. The Queen Regent had gone mad. She'd already thrown that young fellow Jandilay into the dungeon. I couldn't let her arrest the whole theater company, so I ordered the gatekeepers to let everyone out of the city."

"And we convinced him to come with us," said Drax. "He's not the most promising recruit we ever had, but we'll teach him our trade."

Evington knew he had unfinished business. He knelt before his royal brother. "I ask your pardon," he said humbly.

"What for?" asked Evardo. "For helping these rebels escape?"

"No! That's the best deed I ever did and I'd do it again ten times over. No, it's everything else that I'm ashamed of. I had nothing to do with Eviret's sleeping spell, but I did a lot of other things I knew were wrong. Can you ever forgive me?"

Evardo forgave him at once, and promised to treat all the royal guard with mercy.

"Now I suppose we'd better turn this caravan around," he told the Mongos. "Eviret is gone. The city will welcome you home. I just hate to see all of you pulling these heavy wagons. Somebody harness me up! I'll pull one myself."

At this, Onna Val spoke up again. "That reminds me of something else. Where's Button-Bright? Button-Bright, get over here, will you?"

The two boys had hung back while the Evites sorted themselves out. Now they stepped forward. "What's up?" asked Button-Bright. "Are we in trouble for bad diplomacy?"

"No, no," Onna Val laughed. "I want you to hear what Lurline told me. Drax and Ridj, you should hear this too. And King Evardo. Here's the thing: Lurline said Button-Bright could restore the Wheelers to their original forms."

Everyone fell quiet. All the Wheelers drew close.

"What do you mean?" asked Drax.

"Is that even possible?" asked Evardo.

"No more wheels!" said Onna Val. "Lurline said so. Button-Bright, what do you think?"

Surprised to find himself center stage, Button-Bright explained about his Yookoohoo powers. "It's just transformation," he said. "I do it all the time."

"Can you break a spell as powerful as this one?" Ridj asked doubtfully.

"I don't see why not. You see, it isn't really a spell. It's just a form you've been given, and forms can be changed. I change mine and Ojo's five or six times a day. So long as I know what I'm turning you into, there should be no problem."

"It's true," Ojo testified.

"He changed Fluff and me into swallows," said Bud.

"And back again," said Fluff. "It didn't hurt a bit."

"Just don't try his magic food," advised Onna Val, winking at Button-Bright. "Things that taste good aren't his strong suit. What he *is* good at is any kind of living creature."

Drax and Ridj looked at one another. Then they looked at the assembled Wheelers. There were dozens of them. Some still wore their harnesses. Others had just crawled out of the wagons and stood stiff and squinting under the morning sun. The luckier ones had spent the last three years working for the Royal Theater, concealing their real expertise, while the rest had drawn carts and carriages for hard-hearted masters. As they realized what Button-Bright's offer meant for them, their expressions ranged from joy to wariness to outright hostility.

"If it's true," said one, "it's the best news I ever heard."

"I don't see anything good about it," said another. "Why can't we get a little respect just as we are?"

"That's right," said a third. "We're Wheelers. We don't want to be human."

"But we *are* human! Even though we have wheels instead of hands and feet, we're still just folks. Changing back won't change who we are. It'll only change what we can do."

"It'll change what we wear, too. Don't you want to get out of these abominable clothes and these degrading ruffs?"

"And live like normal people again?"

"I never even want to *see* a normal person again! Normal people are cruel, savage slaveowners. Wheelers for the Wheelers! We need a country where we can be ourselves."

It seemed plain that there was no consensus among the Wheelers. Ridj Mongo listened for a while, then turned to Button-Bright. "Thank you for your offer," he said. "We need time to think it over and decide among ourselves. There's no hurry, is there?"

"No. Well, yes." Button-Bright scratched his head. "Come to think of it, Ojo and I have urgent business with King Bud. Urgent for us, anyway. And after that we have to get home to Oz as quick as we can. But we'll be back."

"We're in and out of Ev all the time," said Ojo.

Button-Bright nodded. "Besides, I'd never transform anybody who didn't want to be transformed. That's not the Yookoohoo way. If you're happy the way you are, you have nothing to fear from me."

The Wheelers nodded their heads in agreement. Most did seem inclined to think it over. Drax Mongo, however, rolled toward Button-Bright. "You two boys are best friends," he said. "Aren't you?"

"Of course we are," said Button-Bright. "I wouldn't last two minutes without Ojo."

"Button-Bright is the best friend anybody ever had," said Ojo.

Drax smiled. "I thought so. You have that look about you. I have a best friend too. That's Halvan, who's kept me safe for the past three years. You might say we have a partnership. But what kind of partnership is it when I'm like this? I can't put my arms around him. I also can't pound a nail into a set piece or even write down a single word of my own plays."

"Your plays are right up there with the best," Halvan told him loyally. "And you're a great director, too. Wheels or no wheels, Drax, you're the soul of our theater."

Drax smiled up at him. "Perhaps. But I want to stand up on my own two feet, right next to you, and work with my own two hands. Button-Bright, please change me right now. If it works—and I trust it will—the rest of my people will know what their choice is."

"Are you sure, brother?" Ridj asked him.

"I don't want to wait another minute."

The boy knelt before him. They conferred in whispers. After a moment Button-Bright stepped back and focused his full attention. Everyone held their breath. Could the power of the Magic Egg be overcome so easily?

It could. In an instant Drax stood upright, just as he had wished. His wheels had vanished. And Button-Bright hadn't finished yet. He went on to transform the gaudy clothes into a plain jerkin and leggings and the hated ruff into a loosely knotted scarf. Drax gazed in awe at the hands and feet he hadn't seen in more than two-hundred years. He wiggled his fingers. He laughed out loud.

"You did it!" he said. "You kind, brilliant, miraculous boy! You did it." Then, for the first time in his life, he opened his arms and embraced the delighted Halvan.

Two dozen more Wheelers decided to undergo the transformation as well. All these met with the same success and were joyfully congratulated by their friends. Other Wheelers voted to weigh their options, while some vowed that they'd stay as they were. Now, at least, they had a real choice and knew that their days of servitude had ended. There was joy and relief throughout the whole tribe.

"Now let's all harness up!" cried King Evardo. "Back to Evna!"

"And *we've* got to have our talk with King Bud!" Button-Bright whispered to Ojo.

CHAPTER
TWENTY-SEVEN

TWO
TORTOISES

The sun shone bright over Grandma Natch's house. Even though all had ended well and the boys were coming home with good news, they felt anxious as they flew down toward the clearing. The whole adventure had taken far too long! Would Dame Zanket still be sitting in Grandma Natch's rocking chair? Would Grandma Natch ever forgive them?

There had been one delay after another. It would have been unthinkable to leave Evna before making sure that Jandilay and Onna Val were settled, especially since Jandilay had spent a day in the dungeon. He had come out shivering but otherwise intact, and the happy outcome of his Ev adventure had more than made up for any unpleasantness. The Mongo brothers had confirmed him and

Onna Val as production intern and choral apprentice at the Royal Puppet Theater. King Evardo had warmly endorsed these moves and had even gone on to proclaim that he welcomed all Ozites to his country, both retroactively and for the foreseeable future.

"My family will always be grateful to Oz," Evardo had told Ojo and Button-Bright. "This is the least I can do to honor those who saved my family from the Nome King."

This remark had jogged Ojo's memory. "It's funny you should say that. Ozma decided to celebrate that exact thing. She's putting a festival together right now, with Billina as guest of honor. They're going all out."

Evardo had taken a surprisingly keen interest in this. "A festival? What an excellent idea. Perhaps we Evites can help celebrate. Drax and Ridj, could I talk to you for a moment, please?" He and the brothers had conferred for some minutes. The result had been a marvelous invitation that Ojo and Button-Bright had promised to deliver to their friends in Oz.

A tumultuous Evna welcome had greeted Evardo himself. Few Evites had learned to love the Queen Regent, and news of their beloved king's safe return had spread quickly through the city. Thousands had turned out to cheer the happy homecoming. A few had grumbled upon finding that they'd lost their Wheeler slaves, but the cheers had easily drowned out the grumbles.

CHAPTER TWENTY-SEVEN

In the midst of the celebration, Button-Bright and Ojo had finally managed to corner King Bud and explain the domestic difficulty that had launched them on this journey. The result was that he'd invited them back to Noland—a necessity in any case, since it would have taken him many days to make his way home without their magical help. The three of them had stayed one more night in Evna, enjoying the company of their friends. Jinnicky and Ginger had kept everyone well fed. Return visits had been promised and loving goodbyes had been said. Early next morning, Bud and the boys had taken wing.

In Noland, too, important business had kept them yet another night. All had gone well, however, and Bud and Dab's merry companionship had made the brief visit a treat. If they ever had to live anywhere other than Oz, the boys had decided, it would be right here in Nole.

"King Evardo is noble and good," said Ojo. "But King Bud is all that and fun too."

"A great king and a great friend," agreed Button-Bright. "What could be better?"

More goodbyes had followed next day, and then a flight across the Deadly Desert. Now the Forest of Gugu lay below, richly purple and lavender under the clear blue sky. The wanderers were almost home.

"Let's do a little fly-over," Button-Bright suggested nervously. "Might as well see how bad it is before we face the music."

Down they flew over Grandma Natch's house.

At once they noticed that the rocking chair stood empty. What did this portend? Furthermore, no human presence of any kind was in evidence. Or was it? A sudden shriek of laughter met their avian ears.

"Where did that come from?" whispered Ojo. Button-Bright didn't know. They perched above the verandah and surveyed the scene.

In the middle of the clearing they saw two strange shapes sunning themselves. These appeared to be huge tortoises, as big around as hassocks. Their wrinkled heads wagged back and forth as they gossiped in oddly familiar voices.

"No, no beau of mine ever did *that!*" cackled one. "But my eldest daughter's father was quite a scamp. He came from the great outside world, indeed he did."

"Fancy that!" croaked the other. "The great outside world. However did you understand one another? Why, a person like that might do anything. If you told him to wash the dishes, he might only wipe them instead. And then if you had to eat off the dirty dishes, you both might catch some terrible disease. And then if there were no doctors, you might perish in agony!"

"Dame Zanket, you *want* to perish. You said so yourself."

"True, true. But not in agony. Mild discomfort will suit me just fine."

"My boys will see to it, oh yes they will. Meanwhile, back to that old beau of yours. You say he used to do what for a living?"

This was quite enough for Button-Bright. He had no wish to learn what any old beau of Dame Zanket's had done for a living. He flew down, followed by Ojo.

"Grandma Natch!" he said accusingly. "What have you done to Dame Zanket?"

Both tortoises burst into loud cackles. They sounded like a pair of gleeful witches.

"I haven't done anything to Dame Zanket," Grandma Natch said. "She said she was tired of being an old lady with creaky joints. Who wouldn't be? So I thought to myself, the tortoise is a creature that's in its full prime at eighty or ninety. Let her try that on for size."

"And Dame Zanket agreed?"

"I did!" snapped Dame Zanket. "Very comfortable it is, too. It's the best I've felt in two hundred years."

Ojo didn't know what to think. "So you've changed your mind about leaving Oz, Dame Zanket?" he inquired faintly.

Dame Zanket rolled her small, round eyes. "I said no such thing!" she rasped. "If you're trying to get out of your duties, young man, it won't work. This is a temporary solution to the problem. It's your job to get me out of Oz!"

"Quite right," said Grandma Natch. "Now, what do you two have to report?"

Button-Bright tried not to be unnerved by those two pairs of eyes boring into him. Thank goodness he and Ojo had good news!

Together they told the tortoises what King Bud had shown them in Nole: a large, spacious, sunny estate built just for old people. Such estates dotted the Noland countryside, for King Bud refused to let anyone retire in loneliness and poverty after a lifetime of hard work. The original plan had been hatched by his late aunt. She had known exactly the kind of place she herself wanted to retire to and had decided that everyone should have the same opportunity. King Bud had immediately seen the value of this. In order to make it happen he'd dug into his magic purse and hired a small army of designers and builders, as well as craftsmen beyond count. A whole network of retirement estates had been built. There were two such estates in Nole alone, and a room in one of them had already been prepared for Dame Zanket. King Bud had even been warned about Dame Zanket's eccentricities. Whatever these might be, he had said, the estate staff had no doubt encountered worse.

"So that's it," Button-Bright finished. "We can take you there whenever you're ready."

He and Ojo waited anxiously. What would Dame Zanket say?

She produced a few half-hearted objections. She wouldn't have been Dame Zanket if she hadn't. Were the beds soft and warm? Were there enough bathrooms? Did the staff know how to cook? Would there be a suitable doctor? The boys reassured her on every point. After a final breathless hush, she raised her leathery head and began to cry.

Grandma Natch was alarmed. "What's this?" she said. "Have you changed your mind? Would you rather stay?"

But Dame Zanket shook her head as vehemently as a tortoise can. "That's not it," she said. "It's just—well, it's a dream come true. I do believe I'm actually happy! Thank you so much, all of you!"

The boys had still more good news. "You're both invited to Evna next week," they announced solemnly.

Grandma Natch squinted at them. "What do you mean? Who invited us?"

"King Evardo invited everyone," Ojo told her. "All our friends at the Emerald City, my parents and Unc Nunkie, King Bud, the Red Jinn—all of us. It'll be a huge event. Please say you'll come. I promise you'll have a wonderful time."

"A wonderful time doing what? What on earth is the occasion?"

The boys grinned at each other. "You'll find out when you get there," they said.

CHAPTER TWENTY-EIGHT

THE CURTAIN COMES DOWN

ever before had such an extraordinary audience graced the Royal Puppet Theater of Evna—and what was even more exciting, many of the celebrities would see themselves and their deeds represented onstage that very evening! Evites in the seats below could not keep their eyes off this wondrous assemblage.

In the box just right of the Royal Box sat Princess Evanna and Ridj Mongo, accompanied by a newly shampooed and brushed Cowardly Lion and Hungry Tiger. Both of these great beasts had accompanied Ozma on her long-ago mission to rescue the royal family of Ev, but the prospect of seeing themselves onstage struck each one differently.

"Who ever imagined I'd be played by a puppet in a musical extravaganza?" the Cowardly Lion asked nervously. "I'm terribly afraid that my character won't be a success."

"*I'm* afraid there won't be enough food at the intermission," yawned the Tiger.

Evanna laughingly assured them that they would be both well loved and well fed by appreciative Evites.

Three Americans happened to be sitting in the next box. Two of them, Tiny Trot and a peg-legged old sailor called Cap'n Bill, hailed from the coast of California. The third had been a raggedy tramp when Dorothy first met him in Kansas, and although he now wore silks and satins on state occasions, he still went by the name Shaggy Man. None of these had been along on Ozma's Evite expedition, but the fourth occupant of their box had. This was Tik-Tok the copper man, a marvelous machine who had been manufactured right here in Ev. Trot kept Tik-Tok tightly wound so that he could enjoy the performance.

Three more Americans sat in the next box: two girls called Jenny Jump and Betsy Bobbin and a mule called Hank, who had been Betsy's protector through many perilous adventures. With them were the good-natured Woozy, a quaint beast with a body composed entirely of squares and rectangles, and a considerably less good-natured beast most often referred to as the Glass Cat. She sat on the very edge of the box where everyone could admire her spun glass figure, as well as the pink brains and ruby heart clearly visible within.

"You won't be so smug when you fall into the Orchestra and break," Jenny Jump warned her. But vanity won out and the Glass Cat remained where she was.

Holding court in the next box were Grandma Natch and her spiky-haired daughter Yada, both resplendent in Gillikin purple. Yada Natch had agreed to come only after persistent pleas from her son Button-Bright, and then with the greatest reluctance. Now that she was here, though, this most reclusive of Yookoohoos seemed endlessly amused by the other two occupants of their box.

One of these was none other than Dame Zanket. Button-Bright and Ojo had brought the old lady all the way from her new home in Nole, where she had settled in quite comfortably. She remained stubbornly herself. "Those stage lights are bound to be too hot," she fretted. "If they catch fire, the whole theater will burn up. And then if there's a huge panic, we'll all be trampled to death. And with all these kings and queens and princesses here, there'll be no one left to run things. I tell you it's the end of the world!"

"In that case, kiddo," said the fourth occupant of the box, "let's you and me just sit tight in our seats and enjoy the hijinks. A show like that has got to be the best in town!" This was a giant rat called Percy, who seemed to have decided that the best way to handle Dame Zanket was to call her bluffs—a method that worked surprisingly well, as it turned out. Yada Natch thought it was the funniest thing she'd ever heard.

A very different group sat just left of the Royal Box. The sole Ozite was Scraps the Patchwork Girl, who had Ojo to thank for the brilliantly lunatic quality of her brains. Rarely able to sit still, she turned cartwheels around her companion, none other than the Red Jinn himself. Both were subject to sudden explosions of nonsense verse, and they brought out both the best and the worst in one another. Jinnicky's delighted har-hars echoed all over the auditorium. Their box-mates, Alibabble and Ginger, could only listen in amazement.

Merriment also prevailed in the next box, which Ojo and Button-Bright shared with their new best friends, King Bud and Dab. More Oz notables were their next-door neighbors: the Highly Magnified and Thoroughly Educated Wogglebug, wearing a brand new waistcoat, alongside the equally brainy Frogman, both valued members of Ozma's council. A less intellectually inclined council member was Ozma's earliest friend and companion, the ever-beaming Jack Pumpkinhead. Not to be outdone by the rest, Jack had carved himself a new head just that morning and looked sunnier than ever. The wooden Sawhorse had no intellectual pretensions at all but took great pride in his status as Ozma's favorite steed.

"I hope the puppet version of me will have good strong hind legs," the Sawhorse remarked. "He'll need them when he kicks the old Nome King."

The last box on that side contained two smiling old folks, Dorothy's very own Aunt Em and Uncle Henry. They hadn't been to a real play since their youth and were very excited to find themselves in such a beautiful theater. With them sat Ojo's Munchkin parents, the rulers of Seebania, and white-bearded Unc Nunkie.

Most glittering of all was the Royal Box itself. King Evardo and Queen Fluff hosted Princess Ozma, at her loveliest in an emerald gown that Glinda had once woven as a birthday present. Around Ozma's waist was the Magic Belt, which had transported all the Ozite guests to Evna and would send them home again at the end of the evening. With them sat Ozma's kindly old father, the ex-king Pastoria, who had brought along his trusty sewing kit and was now mending a small tear in Princess Fluff's sleeve. Glinda chatted with Princess Runa (now officially designated Crown Princess Runa), while Dorothy and the Wizard leaned over the railing and made the acquaintance of Ridj Mongo in the box next door.

"I hear that the Wheelers treated you poorly when you first came to Ev," said Ridj.

"That's true," Dorothy replied. "But they changed when we got to know each other. What about you, Mr. Mongo? Will you let Button-Bright turn your wheels into hands and feet?"

"I haven't decided yet. My brother couldn't be happier, so that's something to consider. On the other hand, I've gotten used to being this way. You might say I'm attached to my wheels. Wizard, what do you think I should do?"

"It doesn't have to be either or," said the Wizard. "Now that Button-Bright's friends live here, he and Ojo will come to town more often than ever. He'll fix any mistakes for you."

At the back of the Royal Box sat two of the most famous and beloved personages in Oz.

"I see we're down for a dance number," said the Scarecrow, examining the cast list. He had been freshly stuffed for the occasion and he crunkled delightfully when he moved. "I hope it will be a comic dance. We'd make a wonderful comedy team, don't you think?"

The Tin Woodman agreed, and added that it would surely make stars out of them. He himself already glittered like a star under the brilliant lamps, for his Winkies had polished his tin body to its highest gloss.

Last but not least, at the very front of the Royal Box, Billina presided as guest of honor. She shone in her favorite necklace and bracelets. Propped in front of her was a copy of the program.

"*The Yellow Hen of Oz*," she read. "Fine title for a play, don't you think, Dorothy?"

Dorothy had to agree. "Who would have thought there were plays about us, Billina? Or puppets made to look like us?"

Evardo overheard this. "There are dozens of plays about Oz," he told them. "And both of you are in many of them. Evites never get tired of their Oz plays. But my own favorite play is *The Magic Cloak of Noland*, which tells how my lovely wife became a princess."

"I like the Red Jinn plays," smiled Fluff. "They have such silly songs."

"Oohh, the lights are coming down," observed Billina. "I declare, I'm as nervous as if I were going onstage myself. Imagine a puppet hen prancing around on that stage! If I have a shred of dignity left by the end, it'll be a miracle."

She need not have worried. Seeing her cleverness enacted before a cheering audience was a treat she never forgot.

Of course her sharp eyes noted many changes to the story. The whole beginning, in which she and Dorothy were shipwrecked in Ev, had apparently been deemed too much for a two hour running time. In this version the pair simply traveled from Oz along with Ozma and her people. "How on earth do they think we got there?" whispered Billina. Tik-Tok was discovered in Princess Langwidere's palace rather than in a chamber of rock, and the Royal Army of Oz had been entirely omitted. "No one will miss them," Billina said approvingly. "Eight generals, six colonels, seven majors, five captains, and one private would clutter up any play."

But the best parts remained intact. Princess Langwidere threw tantrums in her cabinet filled with interchangeable heads. The Scarecrow and Tin Woodman made everyone laugh, to the profound satisfaction of their originals. The Nome King proved a marvelous comic villain. Painted scrims represented his lavishly ornamented palace, an eerie and frightening place where Ozma and her friends were transformed one by one into bric-a-brac. At the center of it all, the Yellow Hen clucked and strutted and eventually conquered with the magic of plain common sense (plus two eggs, strictly fresh and above suspicion). The conclusion was a thunderous chorus for the departing Ozites and the restored Evites.

Even more thunderous, however, was the applause that followed the final curtain. Onna Val, wreathed in smiles, could be seen when the backstage chorus took their bow. Button-Bright and Ojo leaped to their feet and whistled. And to crown it all, the Evites—those onstage as well as those seated in the audience—applauded the real Ozites in their boxes. There was even a standing ovation when Dorothy held up a radiant Billina.

The fuss continued out in the lobby afterward. Copious amounts of food had been laid out on tables (even the Hungry

Tiger had no complaints) and a band played dance music from the show. Everyone chose partners, led by King Bud and Dab. Even Yada Natch consented to waltz with Drax Mongo.

"I haven't danced in centuries," she said tartly.

"Neither have I," said the ex-Wheeler. "Let's make the most of it!"

Ojo and Button-Bright had no interest in dancing. Instead they slipped around back to the Stage Door, where they found Onna Val and Jandilay waiting for them.

"Did we sound all right?" Onna Val wanted to know. "I was so nervous before we started, you wouldn't believe it. Then came our first downbeat and we just did it! I had so much fun. Didn't you, Jandilay?"

Jandilay nodded. "I won't sleep a wink tonight," he said happily. "I'm too excited. What a life we'll have!"

"So will we," said Ojo. "We have so many people to keep track of in so many different places, it makes me dizzy."

Button-Bright counted it out on his fingers. "Emerald City, Seebania, Gugu Forest, Darmina's place, Evna, An— even Noland. King Bud asked us over for a week. Wasn't that kind of him? Honestly, though, I don't know where we live anymore."

"Jandilay and I know where we live," grinned Onna Val.

"And what we'll be doing, too," said Jandilay. "Thanks to you. Say, did you know I've started writing my own play?"

"No!" Ojo and Button-Bright were agog. "You mean a puppet play? What's it about?"

"Lurline comes into it. And so do two of your relatives, Button-Bright. And Magic Eggs and flying clouds and all the rest of it. You'll have to help me with it. Onna Val too."

"Us? Why?"

"Because you three are the main characters! I'm calling it *Time Travelers of Oz*."

"*Time Travelers of Oz*," said Onna Val. "There's some history for you. It'll remind me of what I was like two centuries ago. Hey, let's join the party, all right? I want to dance!"

And they all joined hands and ran off through the night.

MYSTERY AND INTRIGUE IN
OOGABOO

Explore Oz!

The International Wizard of Oz Club

Membership brings rewards:

1. Three issues of the Club's premier journal *The Baum Bugle*, fully-illustrated with rare photographs and drawings, popular and scholarly articles on every aspect of the Oz phenomenon.
2. News in the world of Oz, including annual issues of *Oziana*, magazine featuring new Oz stories, and invites to upcoming conventions where you can meet fellow Oz fans, authors, and dealers.
3. Discounts on Club publications.

Join online at www.ozclub.org
or write:
The International Wizard of Oz Club, Inc.
P.O. Box 721129
Berkley, MI 48072-9998
USA

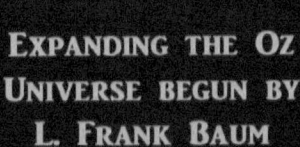